THE
PARTAKERS
WILL YOU TAKE PART?

BRIAR NELSON

TRILOGY CHRISTIAN PUBLISHERS

Tustin, CA

Trilogy Christian Publishers
A Wholly Owned Subsidary of Trinity Broadcasting Network
2442 Michelle Drive
Tustin, CA 92780

Manufactured in the United States of America

10 9 8 7 6 5 4 3 2 1

Library of Congress Cataloging-in-Publication Data is available.

B-ISBN#: 978-1-63769-156-4

E-ISBN#: 978-1-63769-157-1

Dedicated to Jesus, who in the last days will give men and women dreams. To my ever-faithful husband, my proofreader Marah, and all my children, and my Buckeye family who always encourages me in my adventures.

*Character list at the back of the book

CHAPTER 1

And without faith it is impossible to please God.
Hebrews 11:6 (NASB)

Gen walked through the sliding double doors of the East Bank Hospital. The walk from the bus stop was tolerable and she was feeling stronger today than yesterday. "Maybe this procedure isn't even necessary now. This freakin' pain is probably just stress. That doctor barely gave me a second glance. She looked sicker than me," she told herself. But she dutifully walked to the front desk to check in. "Genesis McGuffey. I'm here for an appendectomy."

"What a beautiful name," said the silver haired, young receptionist with a nose ring as she typed at the computer. "Can I see your driver's license and federal medical card please?" requested the receptionist. It was as she handed her the card that her eyes met Gen's for the briefest of moments and then strayed to the strange marking on Gen's right cheek. Though her skin was fair, the burn mark was fairer still. Painted on her right cheek, the burn mark resembled the most amazing appearance of a flower with many petals, delicately drawn on her almond shaped face and then trailed down her neck, under the tight tank top, under her thrift shop denim jacket, and all the way to the tips of her fingers as she handed the receptionist her cards. If she could see further, she would see the scar scratch its way down her side and wriggle its ugly bulges and streaks down her leg to the ends of her toes that protruded from her twisting sandals. There was an awkward smile between the two and a slight look of pity from the receptionist.

Then Gen pulled out a cigarette and started to light up. This immediately interrupted the familiar glance of pity that she despised and turned the receptionist back to her true self.

"Oh my! Miss, you can't light that in here. Those are for in home use only. Surely, you must know this. Please put that away before I have to call someone." She quickly handed her back her cards like they themselves were stained with nicotine. Gen smiled to herself, knowing she doesn't even smoke, but it works every time to ward off looks of pity. Pity is ugly, and self-pity she had learned is far more dangerous than smoking. The woman sized up her small frame and blonde dreads that overwhelmed her size and nodded to the chairs to the left of the check-in and told her to wait for her name to be called.

It was still dark out as Gen stared out the windows and over at the fast-moving Mississippi River that the hospital graced. It raced along at a dizzying pace, smooth, strong and unstoppable. "Miss McGuffey?" beckoned a nurse, covered head to toe in misty, blue scrubs. Gen adjusted the small pouch that hung over her shoulder and across her chest and stood up.

"Genesis?"

"Yes." The nurse's eyes flitted over her eyes and rested on the petals. Gen's gaze fell and she self-consciously looked away.

"This way, please."

Gen grew up south of the hospital in an enchanted suburb called Eden Prairie, where the school district was coveted and the churches had water fountains out front. There were nature walks, colorful parks for children, sprawling miles of malls, and shopping centers, health food stores, and restaurants. Now, at nineteen, Genesis lived four miles south of the hospital behind a tattoo parlor, a CBD outlet, and a new and used tire store.

The nurse and Genesis entered a strangely small and sparse room. Just one chair adorned the corner and a small 18-inch, built-in counter was in the other corner, just small enough to place a laptop computer. As they entered, a young man in all brown scrubs entered discretely behind them. Except it wasn't discretely because the room was now crowded with his hulking presence in the room. Grant tried not to startle when he saw the young woman in the room. It was her. The woman in the vision the Lord had given him. He had been waiting for her. He had searched every stranger's face hoping to find her, and there she was right here in his room! He felt this immense urgency to protect her. He couldn't believe God had brought her right to him. It was her, right down to the dreads that dangled around her face. He attempted not to look at either of them but instead fixed his eyes on the wall ahead of him.

"What's he doing here?" asked Gen, a little suspicious.

"Could you please have a seat?" responded the nurse, clearly ignoring her question.

Gen sat down. The nurse adeptly took her temperature and blood pressure without a word and then looked at the man with a knowing glance and left the room.

It was almost imperceivable, but there was the slightest click. Gen looked at him and their eyes locked. He had heard it too. She looked at the knob and then back at his eyes and his eyes softened. At that moment, she moved toward the door, and he stepped slightly in front of it. His golden, brown eyes searched her eyes until she had to look away uncomfortably.

"The nurse will be right back," he said, trying to sound disarming.

"Well, I have to go to the bathroom," Genesis informed him.

She tried to breach him to get to the door and found herself flush against his chest and his hands gently grabbing her arms. "There will be time to go to the bathroom before the procedure."

As she breathed in his earthy cologne, she noticed her heart quicken. She glanced at his name tag hanging loosely around his neck on a lanyard. She reached for it brushing her hand against him and read the tag aloud. "Grant, it says here that you are an orderly, not a guard, so if you'll please excuse me."

"I can't do that. Not just yet. You'll have to listen to me." His heavy, dark brows furled.

"Okay. You are scaring me. I'm going to start screaming, Grant, if you don't get out of my way. You seem like a nice enough guy, but you are going to lose your job if I scream." She said this as firmly as she could, but her voice shook noticeably as she spoke.

Grant bent slightly and searched the darkest eyes he had ever looked into and blinked so as not to lose himself completely in them. Then, almost pleadingly, replied, "It's my job to stop you from leaving, and I will stop you from screaming."

Gen stepped back two steps. Her head began to swim, and her pulse was now racing. Then she remembered the glance the nurse gave the orderly, the lock clicking, this peculiar room. She pulled nervously at her large bun of dreads. She had heard rumors about this kind of thing. Reports on the web that were up for an hour then pulled as anti-government news. People at hospitals, schools, military and work trips just disappearing. Why? What was the connection? She searched the floor for an answer. And all the pieces began to come together: Ints, Christians. That was it: she was here to be eliminated, or as they say, "repurposed for the greater good."

She looked up at Grant, her eyes wide in wonder, and she knew in an instant. "Yes." It wasn't her voice, but this familiar voice of love and grace from deep inside her. She knew why she was in this room, and it was not for an appendectomy. She was here because she was an Int, an intolerant, a Christian. She wanted to scream, but she couldn't. Her mind began to race. "I'm not strong enough. I don't want to die. Why is this happening to me? I deserve this. I deserve to die. I should have died when they did." She dropped to the floor and wept. She wept for all the lost years, the pain she suffered. The loneliness and hopelessness enveloped her.

This is not what Grant expected at all. He looked at her helplessly. But she continued like he wasn't even there. In her weeping, he saw her great loneliness and sorrow. Finally, he knelt and scooped her up in his arms. She pushed his head back and kicked him away only to have him bundle her up in his strong arms again. Her cheek brushed against his short whiskers, and she buried her head in his neck. The tears and the memories flooding faster than she could control them. "Why are you doing this? Why?" She uncurled from him and waited for an answer. He glanced at the fullness of her lips and looked into her eyes and lost himself completely this time. He grabbed her face with his hands and wiped her tears from her face. He drew her closer and began to kiss her. She melted into him in her sorrow and found peace in the warmth of his kiss. He leaned into her and kissed as though he had been waiting years for this. His arms wrapped around her back and Grant prayed God would slow his passions.

Just then, the door flew open, and the nurse was glaring down at Grant. "What in the world are you doing?" she demanded in disgust.

As he got up, he whispered in her ear ever so slightly, "Listen." Then straightening up and glaring at the nurse, he said, "Well, you can't blame me. It's not like anyone's gonna care."

"Well, we'll see about that! Follow me!" She rushed out the door with Grant in tow and disappeared without a glance back. "Dr. Houston! I want to report..." and the door closed shut.

Gen stood there, her mind reeling like a fishing string being pulled out to sea by a very large fish at risk of never stopping. "What just happened? What is happening? Do I know him? It feels like I know him. Listen?" She stood there and grabbed her head with both hands and forced silence between her ears so she could just think and listen, listen. "Go, go, go." It was deep down. The voice of the one who knew her better than herself. She inhaled and walked to the door, turned the knob, and pushed the door open in faith. She turned away from the cluster of chaos that Grant was now the center of.

She walked as though she was invisible down the hallway. "Up." And there was the staircase. Up one floor, then two, her breath was heavy. Up three, then four. A door stood in front of her with a window and an alarm. "For Emergencies Only" was written in red across the push bar. She looked through the window out onto the roof and again at the door warning. "Please, Jesus," she whispered. And she opened the door in faith and silently stepped out onto the roof. "Flowers." Flowers? Panic and doubt swept through her like a rough current. "I'm on a roof! There aren't any flowers on a roof!" Gen swiped angrily at the loose dreads dangling in her face and began to search the roof for flowers. There, at the entrance to the hospital, the roof was layered in flowers. Beautiful flowers. She must have overlooked them in the dark morning hours. The steps that would lead to her freedom were laid out before her, prepared decades earlier to make the hospital more welcoming for the hurting. She walked her way down floor after floor. The sun was high in the sky now, lighting up the parking lot below.

She saw people entering and exiting, and not one noticed the small framed, dreaded girl weaving her way down the angular, flowered roof of the hospital. No one, except the young silver haired receptionist with a nose ring, who was looking directly at her. She was standing in the parking lot beside her red convertible sedan. Its top was down, and two young men were in the back seat. Gen hesitated and listened once again. Nothing. Should I run? Wave? Turn back? Continue downward? She listened, then in frustration continued with the most direct route to freedom. She came to the final tier of the flower beds and looked over the edge. No one anywhere but the receptionist looking impatiently right at her. She bent down and hung her feet over the edge of the roof. It was still a good twelve to fifteen feet off the ground. She swung her pouch around to her back and spun around and slid off the edge, hanging for a moment by her fingertips. Then, in faith, she let herself fall to the ground. She splattered backwards onto the ground quite ungracefully and whacked the back of her head hard on the asphalt. She stood up quickly, hoping no one saw her catastrophic landing, only to find the receptionist and her two passengers still staring at her blankly. Now what?

"Are you coming?" the silver haired receptionist quipped, impatiently to Genesis. She glanced behind her just to make sure she was talking to her. Genesis walked over to the receptionist, and she said to Genesis, "Get in. We are late." They pulled out without incident, and Genesis watched the hospital, the river, and Grant fading away in the rearview mirror.

CHAPTER 2

*For we have become partakers of Christ, if we hold fast
the beginning of our assurance firm until the end.*
Hebrews 3:14 (NASB)

Gen could feel the eyes of the guys sitting behind her, but she ignored them. She squinted as she inspected the receptionist. Everest swiveled her head to meet her look, her wispy pixie hair flying wildly in the wind. "So, who are you? And what are we late for? And do I know you or something?" asked Genesis.

"My name is Everest. This is Darrell, and that's Lorenzo." Darrell looked at Gen, clearly irritated with her presence, and Lorenzo smiled warmly and lifted his head in greeting. "You, not we, are going this evening to be debriefed by Boxer."

"Boxer?"

"That's what he goes by. No one knows his real name. It's safer that way for everyone," replied Everest.

"So is your real name Everest?" asked Genesis.

Everest rolled her eyes and clucked. "Yes. After Boxer debriefs you, Lorenzo will find you and bring you to a safe room, where you will stay for the night. It's not much, but you'll be safe."

"Woah, wait a minute. Safe? Why? Am I not safe? I wasn't there for a procedure, was I? And who are you people? And I'm not interested in going anywhere. Just drop me off at my apartment, please."

Everest slowed down and came to a stop at a red light. She swung her manicured nails through her hair and looked at Gen sympathetically. "I know this is a lot to take in, but you can't go back to your apartment. You can't ever go back to your apartment, because they know you know too much. They are probably flippin' it right now, and your things will be gone by nightfall. By tomorrow, you will be wiped off any official grid, but you will be forever on their grid."

"Whose grid?" demanded Genesis.

"The United Communist Americas call us Ints or Intolerables. We call ourselves the Partakers. We are on their grid. We are a threat to the peace of the party, according to the UCA."

Lorenzo leaned forward and eagerly added, "Grant calls us the Partakers Party. He says one day we will overthrow the communist party and return to the great nation we once were. But that will take a revolution. Oh, and I like your face. The flower thing."

Darrell jumped in then. "If we ever see Grant again. He's probably being taken in for questioning right this minute. We may never see him again. Where is your faith, girl? You're crying and carrying on 'bout this and that 'bout got us all taken away! What were you thinking?"

"Is Grant in danger?" Gen asked a little too desperately and ignoring Darrell's accusations.

Everest looked her over questioningly. "Grant is smart. And he trusts in God and prays continually. He has been in worse situations, and God's grace has always been sufficient. I think some of us could learn from him." And she turned and glowered at Darrell. She looked back to Gen then turned right into a parking garage and said, "Boxer will know more. When you meet with him, I'll ask him if there's news."

Darrell squirmed a bit in his seat then said, "Sorry, Genesis. I just remember what it was like before Grant came along. We were all on our own, looking out for ourselves, living on fear, not faith. He means a lot to me, to all of us."

Everest pulled the car into a remote corner of the basement of the parking garage. She pushed a button and smooth as a sewing machine the top of the convertible stretched above them, lowered, and clicked into place. "Lorenzo, are we clear?" Everest asked him.

"By the grace of God, yes," he replied with his slight Latino accent.

Darrell gave one more glance to his left then to his right and pulled out a set of keys and opened the eight-foot chain link fence. They walked straight back and entered a storage unit on the left.

"I've got this urge to run, guys," admitted Gen.

"Where would you go that He would not find you? You're here for a reason. At least, that's what Grant said. So, let's see what all that smack is about," Darrell said as he held the door for her.

Everest handed Gen a small, folded piece of paper. Across the top was drawn a three-dimensional box. Then she watched Everest turn and walk across the parking garage and get into a blue Chevy Cruz sedan. She caught a glimpse of Lorenzo around the corner and sat down at a bus stop. Then Darrell said goodbye and closed the door.

Gen noticed she was holding her breath and forced herself to breath in through her nose, out through her mouth. She paused, listening for the voice. Nothing. She saw a 70's style end table with a coffee pot burbling on top of it. She stumbled over a used, woven rug that was held down by a worn, brown, velour couch. "How big is this place?" She whispered to herself. It appeared to be a storage unit, but, as she peered around the corner, she saw a large open space. The concrete seemed to echo her very breath. "What do they need all this space for?" she wondered. She continued walking, her sandals padding noisily on the concrete, when she was approached by the fuzziest longhaired cat she had ever seen. Strangely enough, it swiveled around and in-between her legs purring grandly. She bent and picked up the cat.

"Oh child, you are as beautiful as he said you were. Ah, and the glory of the Lord rests on you."

Startled, Genesis let the cat slip from her hands, and she turned to the baritone voice that addressed her. "You must be Boxer. I have a note for you. And so many questions." She stretched out her hand with the note. The dark, brown man was even smaller in stature than Genesis, although long ago he was probably about her height. His glorious white hair and whiskers made her at ease and even smile for the first time in this very long and trying day. He smiled at her and looked into her eyes and she knew instantly that he loved her. "How did he do that?" she wondered. "It is powerful and beautiful, and I want to learn how to do that." He looked at her scar and followed the trail to her neck and then the hand that she just realized he was holding and then he stepped back and looked all the way down to her toes. When their eyes met, he had tears streaming down his face. He said, "I'm so sorry, child. I'm so very sorry, Genesis."

Filled with a new beauty and strength from deep in her soul she replied, "It's okay. I'm okay. It is well with my soul." He grasped her and held her, and she held him and together they were strong. And, for the first time in a very, very long time, it was well with Genesis' soul.

CHAPTER 3

Wait for the Lord; Be strong and let your heart
take courage; Yes, wait for the Lord.
Psalm 27:14 (NASB)

After Genesis' debriefing, which took many hours because she had many questions, Boxer walked her to the door. As he opened the door, a young boy of only ten or eleven pushed a small, folded note towards Boxer. "Thank you, my son." Boxer laid his dark, knobby hand on the boy's head and mumbled a blessing then tousled his hair. When Gen looked up, the boy was gone and there was Lorenzo smiling back at her. If she needed a bodyguard, Lorenzo would suffice. His bronzed arms and bubbled chest strained every stitch of his thin t-shirt down to his small waist. His cargo pants had a military look to them. If it weren't for that smile, Gen would be terrified of him.

"Just one moment, please," said Boxer. His head, in a naturally downward tilt most of the time, looked at the note with concern. He fumbled to unfold the letter. His lips silently moving as he read. Gen and Lorenzo watched as he read it a second time. Although, both Lorenzo and Gen wanted to ask, "What does it say?" They waited respectfully. Boxer folded the letter and closed his eyes. His silence and stillness indicated he was no longer with them but in the presence of Jesus pleading for direction. When he opened his eyes, he looked at them both. "It is a message from Grant. He has been taken to the Americas Compliance Investigation Center in Minneapolis for questioning." He also said, "To protect the beginning." Both men slowly looked over at Genesis. "Apparently, you make quite an impression on everyone you meet, my dear Genesis," said Boxer with a warm smile. "Lorenzo, please take Genesis to the apartment on fifth. I will get word out to all of the Partakers that we must fast and pray. We will meet this evening as soon as everyone can arrive at our regular prayer location."

"What will we do about the scheduled transfer of the Panthers?" asked Lorenzo.

"That is why we must pray tonight. And of course, for the safe return of our leader," Boxer gravely responded.

Genesis looked at them both incredulously. "I can't just leave! I want to pray! I want to help! It's my fault Grant has been taken. We've got to do something. Who are the Panthers?"

Lorenzo scanned the parking garage for people and nodded to Boxer that we best step back inside. Boxer responded, "Of course, of course." Lorenzo and Boxer sat on the old, brown velour couch, Gen pulled up a chair across from them, and Boxer began.

"The Panthers are the people Grant has found and rescued, who were scheduled for work camp or termination. The Partakers hide them around the city. While the Panthers are in hiding, they train for months, running miles and miles. Then they leave in the middle of the night. They run through woods, over the plains, during the night, for weeks, until they reach the refugee camp in the woods where they live off grid, free, but slaves to the kingdom of God. We are growing in numbers and faith, and we are powerful and ready to be used in mighty ways by our Lord," Boxer said, his voice throaty and strong but still a whisper.

"You were one of those, Genesis. You were scheduled not for an appendectomy, but to have your organs removed and distributed to the tolerant people worthy of life because of their commitment to peace." Boxer continued, "You and your family had been marked years ago as Ints because they were followers of Jesus. They stood against the sins that were destroying our country such as abortion, gay marriage, polygamy. We were labeled bigots, judgmental, intolerant and a threat to our peaceful society. And because of that, the government allowed the rage and hatred against Christians and even Muslims to go unchecked. Christians lost their jobs, they were mugged, beaten, mocked, treated with disdain. At the height of it all, there were riots. Entire families, young people and old were targeted. It was the incidents here in Minnesota, coupled with the assassination of the president and vice president that led to our demise as a nation. In 2020, the woman third in line for presidency stepped into the position of president when our sitting President and Vice President were assassinated. She was a wicked woman. But she reached out to our hurting, divided country as a matronly, loving grandmother. She brought healing and peace and restored order. All the while, she was grooming the next commander of our country: Lady Crestoff. And here we are a decade later: a communist nation. Strong, peaceful, and united to the outside world but lost in sin and wretchedness, secretly destroying anyone who might stand in the way of their utopian peace."

Gen dropped her head, her bun of falling dreads now a mess around her face. "My family's home was destroyed in the gassing of the homes. They filled the homes of believers with gas, and one by one, the homes exploded. I was just arriving home from my friend's house. I grabbed the screen door and opened it. That's when it exploded. I don't remember much else; just leaving the children's hospital with the social worker, the re-educating process, and the foster homes. Then I was on my own at seventeen. I should've died with them, but now I understand. I know Jesus has left me here to accomplish His purposes. I want to work. I want to serve. Please don't send me away."

"You must rest, my child. I'm sure there's much the Lord has for you to do. We will fast and we will pray all night, but we will not move ahead without the Lord. We will wait on Him. And you will rest. Most of our people are at their jobs. They will get the message and will meet us after work." With this, Boxer looked at Lorenzo and they both rose. Genesis kissed Boxer on the cheek and embraced him.

"Come on, little sis," Lorenzo said gently. Then Gen and her capable escort left for the apartment on Fifth Ave.

CHAPTER 4

*Therefore let us draw near with confidence to the
throne of grace, so that we may receive mercy and
find grace to help in time of need.*
Hebrews 4:16 (NASB 1995)

The ACI building in downtown Minneapolis was an old Catholic school that had long been shut down and was now repurposed for investigations into people who were a threat to the people's peace. Basically, where they interrogated possible Ints. The Vietnamese man in military Khakis was dwarfed in Grant's shadow, but clearly, Grant was in his custody, judging by the officer's sidearm and AR-15 slung around his back. Grant walked compliantly by the officer's side with his hands cuffed in front of him. Two similarly armed and dressed officers saluted them as they mounted the great stone steps to the beautiful cathedral. The cross, the altar, the pews, and the beautiful stained-glass windows were all destroyed in the riots years ago. It now looked like a luxury office building.

There was no need to go through any security check points. All the guns in the Americas had been confiscated years ago. It took nearly five years to collect all the weapons. First, there was a call to turn in all firearms. Each person was given $300 per weapon, no matter the type or condition it was in. Then, the government went to the registry, and any one not in compliance were visited by the military police. They went to their homes and confiscated the weapons. These citizens were fined $1000 and forced to attend the three-week re-education program which was offered in all major cities. If you resisted, you were sentenced to ten years in prison and five years in work camps followed by re-education before re-entering society. That is, if you weren't shot on sight for resisting. When all the weapons were confiscated, there was a huge national holiday declared called National Street Day. Vendors and artists and carnival rides lined all the streets in every major city and people caroused safely into the wee hours of the night without fear of violence.

Grant and the officer checked in with a receptionist at the far back of the building. Then they entered the school which was once lined with classrooms on each side of the hallway. Grant looked at the tiled floor as he earnestly sought God's favor and protection in the interrogation that was to come. He recommitted to the Lord that he would give his life for Him. That it was forfeit for the will of the Lord. He pleaded with Jesus to give him the grace to stand up under whatever persecution he might have to face. The officer looked over at him and glared. "What are you doing? Mumbling like an old fool," said the officer.

"Just admiring the fancy tile you put down here. I suppose you didn't do it, though. You just forced some shmuck to do it. I gotta get me a couple Ints to do my work for me. If there are any left," said Grant.

"You are an insolent fool. I have no idea why they employ you. I hope you choke and die on your words in here," the officer seethed.

They entered a room about half the size of a classroom. It was warmly decorated with grand windows framed with heavy curtains. Large paintings of scenic landscapes and beautiful wooden bookshelves filled with plaques, certificates, books, and vases filled the walls.

A large wooden desk, that appeared as old as the cathedral, sat amidst this elegant office that no longer bore any resemblance of a classroom. The officer saluted and greeted the woman behind the desk. He then, quickly retrieved a metal folding chair that looked completely out of place in this office and placed it directly across from the woman behind the desk.

"Sit," ordered the officer. Grant sat in the metal folding chair, and the officer stood to the right of him.

Leisurely, the woman closed her laptop computer and looked up directly at Grant; still not acknowledging the officer whatsoever. She was classically beautiful, despite her bland Khaki uniform. Her hair was pulled back in a bun and parted with precision. And her eyes looked right through Grant, not to his soul but past him to her ambition that laid beyond him. But first she would have to deal with this nuisance.

"Grant Panther," she said slowly and without emotion.

"Miss Arson," Grant repeated back in a slightly mocking tone. The punch from the officer came swift and glanced off of his cheekbone, slicing the skin under his eye. Grant sat back up, straightening himself on his chair once again.

"Do not speak to Major Arson unless spoken to. And you will address her as Major Arson," ordered the officer.

Major Arson continued on seamlessly. "You have been under our employment for six years. I wouldn't call them an outstanding six years. You spent two years as an undercover guard at an elementary school as a substitute teacher before you were accused of protolyzing by a fellow teacher. You convinced us otherwise and dutifully did your re-education before being moved to another school. There you managed to stay for four years before being accused of hate speech against one of our most beloved teachers. She testified that you repeatedly interacted with her as a man would with a man and thereby demeaning her choice to become a woman. But there wasn't much evidence. That was your second re-education which you passed again with flying colors. So now I am looking at your brutish face once more. You are currently assigned as an undercover guard as an orderly at East Bank Hospital. Since you've been there, Mr. Panther, you've lost track of three of the patients you were supposed to be guarding and were caught sexually assaulting the last patient."

At this, Grant released a small chuckle and a smirk. The officer beside him placed the punch this time squarely on his jaw. His face whipped violently to the left. He lifted his cuffed hands to wipe the blood off his lip while his tongue searched for any missing or loose teeth. His dark wavy hair was now sticking to his sweating forehead. He turned his head to the officer and cocked one brow as though to dare him to do it again.

"Do you have an excuse for any of this?" asked Major Arson.

"She clearly wanted me, Major Arson," Grant responded nonchalantly. "And who cares? She's as good as dead anyway. If that nurse wouldn't have walked in no one would have known any better. It's her fault the girl escaped."

"It was your job, sir. And you failed," Major Arson replied.

With that the officer swung his AR-15 around and squarely slugged Grant in the gut with the butt of his gun. Grant felt the air leave his lungs, and then the legs of the chair flew out beneath him. The officer was on top of him, wailing away at his face before he could even get his arms up and finished with several kicks to his kidneys.

"You will be assigned your final re-education class, Mr. Panther. Where you will learn that you will treat all human life with dignity to the very end of it. Then you will be reassigned to the children's wing at UMMC. And if you lose another patient, or sexually assault a child..."

Grant interrupted with a, "I'm not into kids like Officer Wing Wong here is."

This was met with a series of merciless hits to the head from the butt of the officer's gun. Grant laid on the floor motionless, struggling to maintain consciousness, trying to focus on what was being said.

"As I was saying, if you lose another patient or sexually assault a child, it will be you going in for a procedure, Mr. Panther, instead of your patients."

With that, Major Arson picked up her laptop, stepped over Grant's body, and exited the room.

CHAPTER 5

For our struggle is not against flesh and blood, but
against the rulers, against the authorities, against
the powers of this dark world and against the
spiritual forces of evil in the heavenly realms.
Ephesians 6:12

Lorenzo parked the car a mile away from the destination. He got out of the red convertible and began walking towards the park. A couple minutes later, Gen got out and followed at a distance. Gen was thankful for her denim jacket. The air was crisp, and she pulled it closer around her. Anticipation tingled through Gen's body. She had never felt more alive than she had these last twenty-four hours.

As the path neared the outskirts of some trees, Lorenzo stealthily ducked into the forest. Gen did her best to mimic his movements. Genesis followed closer to Lorenzo in the woods as they continued to walk on in silence. The park had a dense core of cedar and pine trees that grew wild and large on the east of Cedar Lake. As they drew deeper into the forest, a beautiful sound began to rise all around her, and she paused in wonder.

She saw Lorenzo grab a stump and sit down, bowing his head in prayer. Genesis just stood in awe of the mysterious voices around her lifted in prayer and praise and song. They were rich and bold. She heard men and women and even a child's voice behind her. There must have been a hundred or more people here. Jesus' sweet presence was so apparent Genesis couldn't help but lift her voice. Her voice was strong, and her distinct melody rose above the rest, as the songs that carried her through her trials in life, carried her to Jesus' throne that night where she was overwhelmed by his love and grace. At times, she fell in His presence and prayed in earnest for this new people of hers. She prayed for Grant and his quick release, his safety, and God's will to be done in his life. She prayed for Darrell and Lorenzo, Boxer and Everest.

As the heavy forest began to shed the first lights of the new day, Genesis looked up to see people moving. She rose from the ground. Lorenzo walked towards a large stump and dropped a folded piece of paper into the hole of a rotted stump. She watched as a few others did the same. Just then, a hand grabbed her hand and squeezed. She turned and saw the wispy silver hair of Everest breeze by. The warmth of these people was intoxicating, and the intense time with Jesus filled her soul. She was ready for work.

Major Arson gracefully climbed the stone steps of the Americas Compliance Investigation Center. She walked blindly by the officers who greeted and saluted her. She unlocked her office and ordered her secretary in.

"What did I have on my schedule today?" Major Arson asked as she opened her laptop and sat down in one graceful motion.

"A meeting with the Lieutenant Commander Brice and three interrogations," replied the secretary, willing herself not to make eye contact with Major Arson for fear of the wrath it might bring.

"I need my calendar cleared. Arrange dinner at The Banks with Lieutenant Commander Brice for this evening. Push all three interrogations to tomorrow," ordered Major Arson.

"What would you have me do with the four interrogations scheduled for tomorrow, Major Arson," asked the secretary, gingerly.

"Would you like me to do my job and your job as well?" Major Arson replied condescendingly, without giving her a glance.

"No, Major Arson. I'll take care of that immediately. Anything else, Major Arson?" asked the secretary.

Major Arson simply "tsked," and the secretary quickly exited.

A few minutes later, against her better judgement, the secretary entered once again and announced, "Officer Wong is reporting for duty, Major Arson," then opened the door wider and allowed him in the office and closed the door behind him.

Without looking up, Major Arson said, "Officer Wong, stand at attention."

Officer Wong quickly obeyed. He stood there before her with his chin slightly raised and eyes forward. His black boots were polished, and his uniform was pressed. His gun was cleaned and holstered to his side with his AR-15 swung around on his back.

"How long have you worked for me?" Major Arson asked.

"Eighteen months, Major Arson," Officer Wong replied.

"Remove your weapons, soldier," Major Arson said as she efficiently rapped on her computer.

"Yes, Major Arson," he replied. Officer Wong lifted the AR-15 over his head and rested it on the wall. He then removed his Glock and holster and placed them beside the other weapon. He returned to attention without so much as a flinch.

"Remove your boots, soldier," Major Arson said.

"Yes, Major Arson," he replied.

She studied Officer Wong as he removed his boots. Then he returned with a completely blank face to attention.

"Remove your uniform, soldier." She studied him as a slight twitch crossed his face. She left her computer open and walked around to the side of her desk.

"Yes, Major Arson," he replied again but not with the crisp sound of duty that was in his other responses.

Officer Wong searched his mind frantically as he fumbled with his shirt buttons. He had been hazed by other soldiers when he first enlisted. It was brutal and personal. They hated him for being Asian, small of stature, a perfectionist, and ambitious, but he was all the stronger for enduring it. It was not much more than he had already endured in his life. He untucked his shirt and removed it.

But he couldn't ever remember hearing of a superior officer being involved in a hazing. He unbuckled his buckle and unbuttoned his pants. But this is so strange. Certainly, Major Arson was stunningly beautiful, cunning, and ambitious. *What do I do? She is ruthless and would never stand for not complying with an order. What is this? What is happening?* And Officer Wong stepped out of his pants and returned to attention.

"Remove your undershirt, Officer Wong," ordered Major Arson as she leaned on the edge of her desk.

Officer Wong's heart raced, searching for any reasonable answer. And for the first time, Officer Wong broke attention, and his eyes swayed to her eyes. And there they stood. For just a moment, he looked into her eyes. And he could see clearly now, it wasn't sexual, it wasn't a hazing, it wasn't even a test of loyalty. He saw darkness, unbridled ambition, rage, and a deep lust for power. Officer Wong was a soldier; dutiful, strong, and loyal, but he faltered at the sight of this in one of his superiors. His gaze returned to attention. He removed his military issued undershirt and stood.

Major Arson threw her head back in a most undignified manner and laughed haughtily in victory. "Go get me the second volume of the Marxist order and *Homo Deus* from the shelf over there."

Officer Wong went to the shelf and retrieved the book but not in his usual purposeful stride. Then stood at attention.

"Get me a cup of coffee," Major Arson ordered.

And so, the day continued. It was only interrupted once when the secretary entered and gasped to see Officer Wong nearly naked, standing at attention before Major Arson. She looked helplessly at Officer Wong, then dropped her eyes and backed out of the room, closing the door.

Late that afternoon, as the sun outside the windows began to descend, Major Arson turned to Officer Wong and said, "I have some things I will be asking you to do in the coming days. I want them done quickly, precisely, and without questions. I have plenty of pictures here of you undressing in my office. They would be tricky to explain if they ended up in the wrong hands, especially if I added any accusations to them. So please do your job well. You are dismissed."

As Officer Wong bent to pick up his clothes, he felt the violent thrust of Major Arson's heel on his backside, and he went sprawling to the ground. She once again threw her head back in a haughty laugh. Officer Wong picked himself off the floor and lamely stood at attention before her.

Major Arson said, "I almost forgot." She went around to the other side of her desk and pulled from her drawer a brass bar. You've been promoted." As she looked him in his eyes, as he gazed straight ahead defeatedly, she moved inches from his face and said, "I will take you with me all the way to the bloody top but don't ever forget who owns you." And with that, she opened the brass bar pins and pushed them directly into Officer Wong's chest. She turned and closed her computer and placed it in a small bag and walked out of the office.

CHAPTER 6

They have become filled with every kind of wicked-
ness, evil, greed and depravity.
Romans 1:29

Major Asia Arson pulled up to one of the many small
government funded homes near the agency and parked.
She walked briskly to the front door and entered. She
unpinned her bun and shook out her long, rich, auburn
hair. She quickly changed into a low-cut, navy dress
with some Michael Kohrs heels and matching bag, then
walked back out the door in less than fifteen minutes
and drove to The Banks where she was to meet Lieutenant Commander Brice.

Asia arrived fifteen minutes early and ordered a
martini, dry, to ease her nerves from the intensity of
the day with Officer Wong. His dignity and career were
now firmly in her grasp, and the next step in her plan
was only a few nights away.

Lieutenant Commander Michelle Brice was a powerful woman and drew attention like a politician. She beamed confidently, smiling at strangers as she approached Asia Arson's table. They clasped hands and smiled warmly at each other. They went on to have a lovely dinner and discuss the politics of ACI, the future demise of the rebel Ints, and various Muslim groups still left to silence. Then they left together for the night.

Asia would only need a couple more nights with Michelle, and she would have all she needed. She will use this sexual enterprise with Michelle to gain access to her true interest: Lady Crestoff, a close confidant of Michelle's. With Michelle's influence, Asia hopes to gain an audience with Lady Crestoff. Then she will reveal to Lady Crestoff her discoveries and conclusions from her recent investigations and propose a way to deal with Ints once and for all.

Two days later, the secretary entered Major Arson's office. The secretary held a thin file between her two small hands. Her hands trembled ever so slightly. She looked at Major Arson and was unable to retrieve the words she intended to say. After an uncomfortable pause, Major Arson quipped, "Have you been able to locate Officer Wong yet?"

"Yes," she said. The secretary's lips appeared to be moving, but no sound was coming out.

"And?" pressed Major Arson.

"He's dead." This came out as more of an accusation than a statement. "They found him this morning in his apartment. He shot himself," she said in a tight, high voice. Her eyes were wide with fear, and her feet were cemented to the floor. She willed herself to step forward and handed Major Arson the file. Then the secretary turned and walked out of the office, out of the chapel and down the street to her car.

"Weak! Everyone here is unbelievably weak!" Major Arson slammed her hand on her desk.

CHAPTER 7

The Lord makes firm the steps of the one who delights in him.
Psalm 37:23

Private Neil opened the door to Major Arson's door. What a horrendous first position. The rumors he had heard couldn't be true. Her petty officer committed suicide, and her previous secretary is AWAL. He took a deep breath, stood at attention and said, "Major Arson, Private Neil reporting for duty. I am your newly assigned administrative assistant. What is my first assignment?"

"Clear my calendar for tomorrow morning so I can attend Officer Wong's funeral. And get me Grant Panther in my office right now. I don't care what you have to do. I want him standing in front of me by the end of the day."

"Yes, Major Arson," replied Neil. She said it with such bravado he almost saluted her. "What an idiot. I'm not going to make it here a week," he thought to himself.

Neil had not had much luck at anything in life, and he was not surprised by this lame assignment. He was a black guy named Neil; not Jermaine or Da'Shawn, just Neil. At a whopping five feet tall and 130 pounds, Neil was often bench pressed in the weight room, the first one flung over the wall in obstacle courses, and the last one included in most recreational activities. But the military was his only option. Science mystified him, math made him cry, and the only thing he could do was read and write. College was not an option for him. Although college was free to all people now in the Americas, his grades in high school tracked him into a skilled trade or the military, and Neil was not mechanically astute. And so, here he was at his first assignment determined to prove himself worthy. "I've got to find this Grant dude," he said to himself.

By 3 o'clock that afternoon, Grant was mounting the steps to the ACI building. He prayed the Lord would protect him. He asked Jesus to make him as wise as a serpent and as gentle as a dove. Just as the Lord was with the Pharisees. "Jesus, use me any way you see fit. I only ask that you make it apparent to me that I might not stumble around in uncertainty and darkness like unbelievers." When he closed out his prayer, he looked up and was standing in front of Major Arson.

Grant swung his hand through his thick dark hair, hoping Major Arson would notice the black eye and bruised jaw. "No handcuffs this time? How pleasant. So, what brings me here today? I was at the best part of the re-education program. The part about freedom of choice. The kinds of choices we are given in this great country of the Ameri—"

Major Arson cut Grant off and said, "I'll get right to the point. I need you to enlist. Officer Wong is gone, and I want you in his position."

"Did Officer Wong have a better off—"

"He's dead," Major Arson paused. "Will you enlist? I'm not going to ask again."

Grant inhaled a prayer and exhaled an answer. "So, you want me to beat the crap out of shmucks like me?"

"You were military once. This is nothing new to you."

"That was a long time ago and in a very different country. Obviously, not as grand as this current one. But didn't you read my file? Not so honorably discharged. Had a small problem with authority, snooping, and I'm a bit of a pacifist. Blood makes me pass out. Apparently, not my own blood," he said with a chuckle. He paused a moment to let that sink in. "But I do think I could continue to offer you my services as a civilian, maybe in a more valuable way. I am a mediocre guard, as you know, but I'm an outstanding private investigator. That's my other job. You're the interrogator, but you need an investigator to find the people to beat up and the dirt to charge them with. If you have good intel there can be less beating and therefore less blood, as I prefer. If you can live with me intimidating them rather than beating them, we might be able to work together."

"I can't pay you unless you're enlisted. I don't have that kind of freedom with funds, yet. But I can get you assigned to me," she said matter-of-factly.

"Hmm. But I'm still tied up with my re-education for another two weeks," he said in mock disappointment. "And I still have a couple of cases of my own that I need to tidy up."

"I'll give you two days to tidy up your personal business. I'll see to it that you've passed your re-education classes, again. Hell, you could probably teach them. Then be back here in my office at 8 a.m. in two days. Private Nate will get your paperwork filed in the meantime."

"Private Neil," corrected Grant. "You do have a way with people."

"When you return, Mr. Panther, you will never correct me again. You will never cross me, speak to me condescendingly, or even look at me. Do we have an understanding? I don't like men, and I like you least of all. Do we have an understanding?"

"Yes, we do," Grant turned and exited quickly because he was afraid he would say something that would curtail this unique opportunity God had given him.

Grant stopped by Private Neil's desk before leaving. "Thank you, Private Neil, for rescuing me from that dreadful, I mean enlightening re-education class," he said with a deep chuckle. "Major Arson said you would be doing my paperwork for me. I really appreciate that. Here is my number if you have any questions, feel free to call."

Private Neil accepted the card with Grant's number on it and said, "Hey, just call me Neil. But not in front of her. Then, you know, Private Neil. I hope I make it here. I sweat every time I have to open that door. The last secretary went AWAL, and the last officer, Officer Wong, committed suicide!"

"What?" exclaimed Grant. He dropped his head in sorrow and grabbed his forehead and whispered a quick prayer. "I'm so sorry."

"I didn't know him. Never even met him before. Lots of rumors going around, but none of it makes sense. Bad vibes around here. I guess you're re-enlisting and going to work here?" asked Neil.

"Yeah," responded Grant, surprised. "How did you find out so fast?"

"Major Arson had me start your paperwork for it earlier today after I located you."

"Hmmmm. Well, I will see you in a couple of days, Neil. I look forward to working with you," and Grant walked out of the building to his car parked on the street.

"I need to go see Dad, right now," he said to himself as he u-turned in the street and headed for the parking garage.

CHAPTER 8

But seek first his kingdom and his righteousness,
and all these things will be given to you as well.
Matthew 6:33

The parking garage had a splattering of cars here and there. Grant recognized most of them. He walked up to the fence and unlocked it and went to the storage unit on the left. The familiar sound of percolating coffee and the musky, brown couch was as he left it several days prior. He heard hushed voices and rounded the corner to the large open area. There was a metal table oddly set up in the middle of the area with six folding chairs around it. He quietly approached. His dad saw him first, and he jumped out of his chair like a young man. "Son! You're home! You're home!" cried Boxer.

"Dad, I've got so much to tell you," Grant said as he embraced Boxer.

In unison, the rest of the chairs all went screeching back on the concrete as they all rose to welcome back Grant.

Darrell ran over and hugged Grant. "My man! They messed you up! Who was it? Just tell me. They're goin' down."

"God handled it already. Revenge is mine saith the Lord. And it is a frightful thing to be in the hands of the living God. I'm very sad about it," replied Grant.

Lorenzo smiled and did a swooping handshake that slid into an embrace with Grant. "Missed you, bro. But we had your back in prayer. And I was keeping everything safe here," he said and gave a slight nod in Genesis' direction.

And there she was, barely visible at the back of the group. Torn jeans and an oversized hoody. Her hair danced around her beautiful face. He drank in her image probably a bit too long because Everest began to complain. "Well, let me say hi and welcome back before you completely forget that I exist," Everest said playfully and gave Grant a hug.

Grant smiled and hugged Everest, then looked back once again at his dad and said, "Could I have a moment alone with Genesis? I have a few things I need to say to her."

Darrell turned to look at Genesis with a twinge of jealousy. Lorenzo started making whooping noises.

Genesis smiled slightly and looked at the ground and shuffled her feet nervously. "Why of course, son," said Boxer.

With that, the large room was suddenly emptied, and Grant and Genesis stood there, three feet apart from each other. Most people would've found the silence and the gazing awkward, but both of them seemed lost in the other's presence. Finally, Grant said, "Genesis, I need to apologize."

She jumped in quickly. "Apologize for what? You rescued me." She paused. "Thank you."

"Did anyone see you leave?" he asked.

"No. It was like I was invisible. Like Peter when he left the prison. I did fall off the roof, but I think it was just my pride and the back of my head that was hurt," she said with a light laugh and a nervous twist of a dread.

Grant took a step forward. "Were you hurt?" he asked, clearly concerned.

"No. But Everest, Darrell, and Lorenzo saw the whole thing. They're never going to let me forget it."

Another pause filled the air. It was pleasant. Neither made any motion to leave or sit down. They just stood there.

She broke Grant's gaze and looked down at the floor. "Genesis." She looked back up at Grant. "I need to apologize for what happened in the room at the hospital. I shouldn't have... I didn't mean to... I was trying to... Let me start from the beginning. I am an undercover guard at the hospital. I pose as an orderly. But really, I'm not either of those things. I am working there to find people like you, Christ followers, who have been identified and are to be terminated. Then I, or rather we, work a plan to rescue them."

"I know. Boxer explained all of this to me. It's wonderful," she said.

"But when I saw you... See, six months ago I had a dream Genesis, and you were in it."

Genesis leaned back a little. "What? Me?"

"You were as plain to me as you are right this minute. I saw every curve of your face, the depths of your eyes, your smile, your hair, and the burn on your face. We were there in the waiting room together. I haven't been able to sleep or focus or work. I've prayed for you and waited for you and looked for you everywhere. I thought I was going to go crazy. And when you walked into that room I couldn't even breath. I couldn't even look at you, and when I did, all I could think was I have to get her out of here. I can't let them hurt her. And all I could think to do was to—" He paused, and his voice faltered. "Kiss you. I'm so sorry," he said as his voice trailed off.

Genesis realized her mouth was slightly open and her eyes were wide. She stepped forward and grabbed his hands and smiled up at him and said, "Thank you, Grant."

She dropped his hands slowly and tilted her head. "So, how exactly is Boxer your Dad? You don't exactly resemble each other."

"Ha!" Grant said. "No, we don't. Both my parents died when I was two years old in a car accident."

Genesis' hands went to her mouth. "Oh, my gosh. I'm so sorry!"

"My father was killed instantly. My mother died two days later. But before she passed, she asked Boxer to raise me. He was a pastor at the church my parents attended. They were very close to him and asked him to raise me as his son in the ways of the Lord. Boxer never married. He spent his life raising me. He's the only father I've ever known, except my heavenly Father. He means everything to me." Another few moments of silence passed. "I have a lot of important things to discuss with the others. Kingdom things. And in these last days that must be a priority. But Genesis, I would love to start over with you. I want to get to know you; everything about you. Do you think that's possible?"

Genesis had gotten lost in his words. Words she had never thought she would hear from someone. Her life was almost over a few days ago, and now it feels like it was just beginning. God is so good. "Yes. I would like that very much."

CHAPTER 9

*The terrible thing, the almost impossible thing, is
to hand over your whole self—all your wishes and
precautions—to Christ.*
C.S. Lewis

At the center of the table was a haphazard pile of folded papers. Boxer bowed his head, and the others followed. His voice rose and fell with his heartfelt words. "Lord Jesus, we are now living in the wicked days you spoke of. Your people are suffering persecution and even death in a nation that once honored you above all else. Have mercy on us, Jesus. Forgive our land for its violence against your people, for the murder of the unborn and the elderly, for homosexuality and all sexual immorality. Forgive us, Lord. Heal our land and restore it to what it once was. Start with us first, Lord. Remove all forms of lust and jealousy, strife and envy. Fill us with Your love. May we bring glory to You, in the way we love and serve each other. Help us to love our enemies. And, Lord, give us the grace to endure all kinds of hardships. May we find joy in our suffering. And lead us, Lord, in Your path. Direct our steps to save Your suffering people. This is our desire and what You have called us to do. And thank You, my precious Jesus, for returning my son and our leader to us so quickly. We praise Your Holy Name, King of Kings and Lord of Lords. Amen."

Several "amens" echoed. And everyone began to shuffle and look curiously at the folded papers. Boxer began again by addressing Genesis. "Genesis, what a joy it was to have you at our gathering to pray and praise and fast. Your voice brought joy to the masses as you lead us in praise. What a gift the Lord has given us in you."

Genesis was shocked. "I didn't even see you there, Boxer. It was so overwhelming, the presence of the Lord, I couldn't help myself. I didn't mean to overstep, if I did."

"Not at all, child. Not at all. I look forward to you leading worship in the future for us here on Sundays. If you will agree to. We have long been waiting for someone to fill this great concrete hall with song."

"Of course. Anything I can do at all," replied Genesis. She caught Grant looking at her with a slight smile of surprise.

"So much more to learn about Genesis," he thought to himself. Then Grant also addressed Genesis and the group. "At these gatherings the Lord has always spoken to our group. And He has never once led us astray. He is faithful at every turn. At the end, if the Lord has spoken to an individual, a message for the group, those people will write it down on paper and place it in the stump. I assume," Grant said looking at Boxer, "these were from the last gathering."

"Yes, yes," replied Boxer, "and let us begin to unwrap the mysteries and adventures the Lord has called us to." Boxer unfolded the first note and read, "Darrell will lead, and Lorenzo will follow." Boxer unfolded another note. "There is a position open for a social worker at Children's Branch at UMMC." Boxer unfolded another note. "Your leader will be put in danger, but I will never leave him or forsake him." All eyes rolled over to Grant. Boxer continued to open the next note. "Your group will be in great peril. Brace yourself." Boxer continued, "The enemy will appear as an angel of light." Boxer continued, "Oh Death, where is thy sting?" Boxer unfolded the final note, "Let the children come unto me."

Grant began to pray. "My Lord Jesus, my friend and my brother. Though we walk through the valley of the shadow of death we will fear no evil. For we have a hope that lies beyond this earth. We will trust in you."

Grant lifted his head. "I'd like to update you on some things. I was let go of my position as guard at East Bank Hospital for sexual assault and allowing a patient to escape."

"What?" exclaimed Darrell. "Sexual assault?"

Everest folded her hands to calm herself.

Lorenzo said, "They're lying."

Boxer said quietly, "Let's let Grant explain."

"I am so sorry, Genesis. I don't want to make you feel any more uncomfortable than I already have, but this must be out in the open or the enemy could take a foot hold through gossip. And I want to in every way take the blame and leave nothing to tarnish your reputation."

Genesis nodded and smiled slightly. "It's okay, Grant. Go ahead and explain."

Grant rubbed his forehead, then ran his hands through his hair and with a deep breath folded his hands in front of him and began. "I want to be totally honest about what happened. I've seen Genesis before in my dreams. Darrell and Lorenzo and Dad know about this because I've shared with them about my dream. When I saw Genesis there in person in the prep room, and I knew they were going to terminate her, I panicked. I had to find out a way to get her out of the room. I was kissing Genesis when the nurse came in the room, and I played it off like I forced her to. The nurse reported me for sexual harassment, and that is when Genesis was able to escape."

An awkward silence filled the space between them all. "I have apologized to Genesis. She has accepted my apology." Everyone glanced at Genesis who nodded in agreement. "But there is more that I have to report. I was interrogated by Major Arson. You are all aware of her unwavering hatred for God's people and the number of people she has had beaten and killed."

"Are those wounds from her, my son?" asked Boxer gently.

"Well, a man named Officer Wong did this at her request. But these wounds are not from him, as you so wisely taught me, Dad. For we do not wage war against flesh and blood but against powers and principalities of the air. I'm not sure what happened after that, but Officer Wong shot himself the next day, and Major Arson's secretary went AWAL. After that, I was sent for the three-week re-education class, but after two days I was removed and sent back to Major Arson's office. She has asked me to re-enlist and take Officer Wong's position."

"What?" exclaimed Everest. "You couldn't possibly do that! It's too dangerous. If she ever found out, she would torture you, then kill you, publicly!"

"You mean like they did to Jesus?" Grant said quietly.

"But we need you. What about the Panthers? The next group is set to leave in two days," replied Everest.

"I think that has already been solved. Darrell will lead, and Lorenzo will follow."

"I'm ready for it, Grant. I know I can do this through Christ who strengthens me. I've gone over the path in my head so many times. And with Lorenzo at the back, it will be no worries," said Darrell eagerly.

"I'm up for it," Lorenzo said with a confident smile. Darrell and Lorenzo slid each other a quick bump.

"I am concerned about the position this will put you in, son. Arson is a wicked woman. She will ask you to do things you will not be able to do."

"And it is then that the Lord will provide for me a way out. I trust Him, Dad. I will have opportunities for the first time to get intel before it's too late. The lives that could be saved, Dad. Not just one by one but families at a time. This is an opportunity we can't pass up. I know He has orchestrated it. We will work on an emergency exit plan. I will be careful and wise."

"Then it is settled," said Boxer.

"Now," continued Grant. "About the position at the Children's Hospital. What an incredible opportunity. Thank you, Jesus. If we find children, we can save the entire family. Do we know anyone not currently employed in our extended group that might want to do this?"

There was a long pause.

"I can do it," answered Genesis. Everyone turned to look at Genesis. "Everyone has always said I have a way with children. I love kids."

"It's just too dangerous. I'm sorry, Genesis," replied Grant with a stern look.

"I don't think it is," retorted Gen.

"You haven't done this kind of undercover work before. I just can't take that chance with you," said Grant.

"I can do this, Grant," she said, still determined.

He looked back at her and smiled. Then he heard the Lord say, "Yes." But Grant ignored that.

"Genesis, they already know what you look like at that hospital. You would be in danger if someone recognized you," said Grant, just as determined.

"I can change the way I look. I am a woman. That's easy for us. And we are all in danger, just being followers of Christ," she said as she sat a little straighter.

"I used to be a hairdresser before all this. I can make you look like a totally different person, Gen," piped in Everest. "It will be fun!"

"What about your scar?" Grant said gently.

"Make-up," she said with a twinkle in her eye.

"Okay, it's done," said Boxer.

Grant held her gaze a little too long until Genesis finally smiled at him reassuringly.

"Most importantly, we will need our people praying. Everest, my prayer warrior. I need a group praying about the angel of light. I need another group praying about the safety of the Partakers and the Panthers. I also need a group covering the children in prayer. The children at the hospital that Genesis will be interacting with and the children that will be traveling with Darrell and Lorenzo."

Everest was quietly scribbling down all this information in a large, hard cover notebook. Its pages were bent and wrinkled and yellowed. Everest caught Genesis staring at it. "It's my prayer journal from this month," she said to Genesis as she pulled an attached string through the book to mark her place.

Genesis said in wonder, "All that from just this month?"

"God and I talk a lot, and I don't want to miss or forget a thing He says or does, so I write it all down," said Everest. "And I'm rather persistent, so I keep going back to requests until He answers them. I think He likes that about me," she said. "Anything else, Grant?"

"No, let's close in prayer. Jesus, my faithful friend, deliver us from the evil one's plans. Keep us strong until the very end. Let us walk by faith and not by sight and hold us in your grace and love."

CHAPTER 10

Truly I tell you, anyone who will not receive the
kingdom of God like a little child will never enter it.
Mark 10:15

Darrell and Lorenzo stood back and observed. Both of them rested on their heels with their arms crossed. Before them, in the lower level of the parking garage, stood God's great people. This group of Panthers would carry twelve souls. This will be the twenty-seventh group to make it to the refugee camp. There were three sets of parents and six children. One of them was only three months old. The others were boys ages ten, twelve, thirteen, and fifteen. Then one girl who was thirteen.

"The baby may be difficult. At a minimum, unpredictable," said Lorenzo.

"Trevor assured me it will be fine. He has been running with weights in his backpack. The mom, Autumn is healthy and strong," replied Darrell.

"How do the kids look?" asked Lorenzo.

"Most of them better than me," chuckled Darrell. "I'm a little worried about the ten-year-old, Judah. That's young. I couldn't have done this at ten."

"So, who belongs to whom?" asked Lorenzo.

"All four boys belong to Ashley and Matthew: Judah, Luke, Paul, and Peter," said Darrell.

"Ha! All Bible names," laughed Lorenzo.

"The girl, Makayla, belongs to Devon and Trina. She's a mighty one, that Makayla," said Darrell.

"Did you notify all the Partakers in Ontario that we are leaving? And have all the vehicles been checked and double checked?" asked Darrell.

"Yes," answered Lorenzo.

Darrell called the small group together for a final meeting before their departure. "As many of you know, Grant has been called to another important task at this time, so I will be leading you to the refugee camp, and Lorenzo will be taking my usual back position. I need to review a couple items before we leave."

"Does everyone have their travel permission slips with them? Please pull them out and make sure that they say Departure: Minneapolis 6/20/2030, Arrival: Thunder Bay 6/20/2030. Each adult and child need to have their own travel permission slip."

There was a rustling of papers. The children began to compare one another's travel papers. Trevor raised his hand to get the attention of Darrell. "I don't need travel papers for Lissa, the baby, right?"

"Yes. Yes, you do. Weren't you able to get her papers?" replied Darrell, clearly concerned as he began to walk closer to Trevor.

"Well, we really didn't want Lissa's name in government files. They don't even know about her. Autumn gave birth to her at home, and I delivered her," explained Trevor.

"At the check points, we will have to give an accounting for the baby," added Lorenzo.

"We will just have to keep her hidden and pray that Jesus will give us protection. But you have put our entire group in danger. The only way we make it to the refugee camp alive is by following what Lorenzo and I say. For all our sake, we need to follow directions. Our individual decisions will affect everyone in this group. If you're not sure about something, ask Lorenzo or myself." Darrell's tone clearly expressed his disappointment.

The group began to look around nervously at each other until Makayla spoke up. "We can do this. I can help. I'm good with babies."

"Thank you, Makayla, and that's just the kind of attitude we are going to all need to get through this. We will need each other to help when we are weak and encourage us when we lose hope. And I need every one of you to do exactly what Lorenzo and I ask you to do. All of our lives will depend on it," said Darrell, while looking each adult and child in the eye.

"Next, I need to remind you that there are no electronic devices. No phones or smart watches of any kind. We are going off grid," said Darrell as his eyes scanned the room, their heads were shaking in agreement.

Lorenzo stepped forward, hands in his pockets. "The only things you are allowed to bring are two sets of clothes, three pairs of underwear, three pairs of socks, one extra pair of shoes, a coat, hat and mittens, and a sleeping bag. The rest of the pack must be used for carrying water and food, which we will provide. We will be sleeping out in the elements, and we will be supplying the sleeping bags as well," said Lorenzo.

"We are hoping to exit the vehicles in six hours. We will not be stopping, eating, or drinking until that point," added Darrell.

Just then, a garage door opened in the far corner, and two grey minivans pulled in. Everyone smiled in anticipation. Grant exited one vehicle, and Boxer exited the other. Grant went over to both men and shook their hands and smiled proudly.

Grant addressed the group about some last-minute procedures. "Check points are random, but usually they are either just north or south of Duluth. That will be your first hurdle. There aren't any check points outside cities, so once you clear that check point you should be good. The peacekeepers only monitor people coming and going from the larger cities. They are looking for anyone with warrants, especially Ints with warrants, and any weapons. They have dogs that circle each car smelling for weapons."

"Since all radio waves have come in under the control of the government as you know, you are more likely to pass the time in the car praying and worshipping for the days are wicked and dangerous for believers to be traveling. Christians are not allowed to gather in groups of more than ten and so you will have to divide into your family groups if you are forced into a public situation. Any questions?" Grant rocked back on his heels and waited patiently. When all remained silent, he motioned for his dad. Boxer prayed a final blessing over the Panthers. Then the Panthers started piling into the vans and getting situated. With waves and smiles, full of nervous anticipation, they drove off.

Before they knew it, they saw the yellow flashing lights on the top of the peacekeepers' car ahead of them, signaling for all cars to pull over for inspection. The government did away with police officers. They were at the center of the civil unrest that begun the fundamental change of the nation. Minorities were sometimes being racially and unjustly targeted by police. There was wide-spread protesting and rioting in every major city in the United States of America. A Marxist political group took advantage of the unrest and used this unrest as a platform to promise equality and justice for every person. The Marxist group was so widely accepted by minorities, businesses, and even churches, that the ideology was easily ushered in after the assassinations of the President and Vice President of the United States.

A peacekeeper approached Darrell's car with a flashlight. Both minivans fell silent, except for the whispered prayers. Darrell's van was inspected first. You could see the officer's frustration as he sorted through seven different travel permission forms. Most citizens of the United Communist Americas had already been chipped and sealed three years ago. A simple swipe with the officer's phone and he would have all the information right in front of him and they would be on their way. But now, the officer would have to record each one of them by hand, into his computer as the line backed further up. The rotund peacekeeper returned with the half folded, half scrunched up papers and distributed them back to each person with a sigh of frustration and a glance at the line that had grown behind them. "You're free to go," said the peacekeeper.

"Thank you, sir," said Darrell politely, "But I wanted to let you know, sir, that the van behind us is traveling with us also."

"How many people are in that car?" asked the peacekeeper, clearly irritated now.

"There are six in that van," replied Darrell.

"That's twelve people all together. And I'm guessing none of them are chipped and sealed either?" asked the peacekeeper, clearly agitated, as his round cheeks became rosier. "Why are all of you traveling to Thunder Bay? Is this some kind of Christian meeting or something? The legal limit is ten of you guys." He straightened up his back and wiped at his forehead.

"Oh no, sir. Some of us are family and some us are friends. We are just going up to stay at my cottage for a weekend."

"Good God. I need to see the deed to your cottage. Tell me you have the deed on you," said the peacekeeper.

"God is good! Look, I have the deed right here!" replied Darrell as he handed it to him.

"Stupid Ints," the peacekeeper muttered. He snatched it from Darrell's hand and returned to his car. Darrell turned and instructed everyone to be praying. Even the children closed their eyes, beseeching God's protection.

When the peacekeeper returned, he said, "Pull ahead and wait there until I have cleared the other vehicle."

"Yes, sir," replied Darrell. Darrell pulled ahead, parked the car and joined the others in prayer.

Lorenzo pulled his minivan forward and rolled down the window. "Let me see your travel papers," the peacekeeper said gruffly. Six papers came out the window. He grabbed them and walked back to his vehicle. When he came back, he handed them the papers. "Okay, you're free to go," said the peacekeeper. And then little Lissa let out a small cry. The peacekeeper turned back with amazing agility for his size. His flashlight came out and was searching the car for the baby, and there it was in Makayla's lap. "Is there a baby in this car?" asked the peacekeeper.

Makayla answered in a little girl's voice, "Yes, there is Mr. Peacekeeper. Her name is Baby Alive. She can cry and eat and drink. She can even pee in her diaper. I just got her for my birthday. She's my favorite doll."

The peacekeeper dropped his flashlight and said impatiently, "Go."

Lorenzo flashed his lights at Darrell, and both minivans pulled away.

CHAPTER 11

The Lord is close to the brokenhearted and saves
those who are crushed in spirit.
Psalm 34:18

Grant walked over and shut the garage door. He turned to walk back to Boxer but saw a young, beautiful woman enter the area. She wore a navy pencil skirt and heels that accentuated her lengthy, slender legs, and a loose, white, long-sleeved blouse that came up high around her neck but left an almond shaped opening on her chest. Her hair was long, thick, and straight with a blunt cut. Her blonde hair swayed as she walked toward them. Her large smile drew them both in, and she looked at them as she arched one of her penciled eyebrows questioningly. "Hi," said Genesis. She looked between Boxer and Grant, who stood silent in front of her. "You guys are making me uncomfortable. What do you think? Do I look like a respectable social worker?" she asked.

"You look like an angel," said Grant, unabashedly.

"You are a delight to look at, and you will be a wonderful social worker," responded Boxer with a smile and chuckle and shuffled away.

Grant stepped closer. Genesis stepped even closer to him, making Grant want to grab her in his arms again. She looked up into his eyes.

"I don't know what to say," said Grant. "You look amazing."

"Say, happy birthday," said Genesis. "I'm twenty today."

Grant looked deep into her eyes and whispered, "Happy birthday, my love," and bent and kissed her.

"This was the best birthday ever," thought Genesis as she warmly accepted her first gift today.

Genesis sat down in front of the Human Relations director at the Children's Hospital at UMMC. She crossed her legs nervously.

"So glad you are working here with us, Genesis. We have a lot of children come through here that are in just awful homes. They are spanked, beaten, and brainwashed. People nowadays. Where is all the peace we preach about all the time? Here are the names of five children currently here. We will regularly give you names of children to investigate. You will need to interview them and their family members, and document what was said and then make recommendations. After that, the state will take action," Mrs. Rueport, the HR lady, paused. "I'm so glad it's not how it used to be. In the archaic days, when a child had to be half dead or in imminent danger before we could help them. If you suspect the child is in danger, or worse yet, they are trapped in a home indoctrinating them with lies of intolerance, where they are beaten or worse for stepping out of line, please don't hesitate to write that in your report. I will back you up."

"Thanks so much for this opportunity, Mrs. Rueport," replied Genesis.

"Please, call me Gretchen. You came so highly recommended from the HR lady, Dianne, at the East Bank Hospital. It made my job easy." She smiled at Genesis and rose to see Genesis to the door, her red curls bouncing as they walked. "Your office is room 023. Bummer you're in the basement, but at least it's quiet. You'll probably spend most of your time in the play therapy center. It's a great place to observe the children. That's in room 108. Let me know if you need anything at all," Gretchen said warmly.

"Thank you," replied Genesis. She left the room and started down the hall praying and thanking God for this chance to help these children.

She walked down a dimly lit hallway to her new office. It was windowless with a metal desk on one wall and a Sauder bookshelf on the other. A beautiful, spring flower arrangement sat beside her computer. She smiled and read the card. "Happy birthday, my love." She smiled and squealed inside herself.

"Secret admirers on the first day. That's impressive," said a warm, deep voice behind her.

She turned to see a small, brown man of Indian descent leaning on a mop. He bent over to grab the trash bag out of her can by the door.

Genesis replied to him, "It's my birthday."

"Oh well, that is special now. You have a very blessed day," he said, with that humorous Indian lilt in his voice.

"Do you know Jesus loves you?" Genesis asked, completely out of the blue.

He paused and looked up at Genesis. "What is your name, young lady?"

"Genesis," she replied.

"Hmmmmm, interesting name. Do you know what happened in the beginning?" He paused for a moment then said, "In the beginning, there was the Word and the Word was with God, and the Word was God. He was with God in the beginning. Through Him all things were made; without Him, nothing was made that has been made. In Him was life, and that life was the light of all mankind. The light shines in the darkness, and the darkness has not overcome it. Is this the Jesus you are speaking of?" asked the man.

"Yes. That was beautiful," she replied. "What is your name?"

"Aarav. And yes, I know Jesus loves me very much. I will pray for you, child. You will need it with such a boldness." He turned and walked away, whistling down the dimly lit hallway.

Genesis looked over the list of names. "Rachel Zimmerman, room 214," Gen said to herself and then turned to go find Rachel.

Gen entered the soft yellow room and saw who she assumed to be Rachel. Her thin blonde hair was matted to her head. She had tubes coming out of her nose and her right arm. Her left arm was in a cast. Gen looked at her chart before she had entered the room. Rachel had a collapsed lung. Her left arm was broken as well as two fingers. Gen had gasped as she read the report. She saw that Rachel was asleep, so she was turning to leave when she heard a little cough. She turned back and Rachel's large almond shaped eyes were open. "Hello, my name is Genesis." She stepped over to Rachel's bedside.

"Are you an angel?" asked Rachel. "Momma says there are angels and that I have my very own. But Mike says there are no such things. He doesn't believe in anything."

Genesis gently squeezed Rachel's hand and said, "Oh Rachel, there are angels. They are in this room with us, right now, and so is Jesus."

"Who is Jesus?" asked Rachel.

"He is God! That's who made you, Rachel. He made the sun, the stars, the grass, and the trees. Oh, he loves you so much, Rachel. He sent me here just to tell you that," Genesis said warmly.

"Are you sure you're not an angel?" asked Rachel again.

"No, angels are spirits. We can't usually see them, but one day we will see them. They love and obey Jesus. He made them too."

"Did Jesus make Mike?" asked Rachel in a small, scared voice, "I don't like Mike."

"Is Mike your momma's boyfriend?" asked Gen.

Rachel shook her head slightly.

"Did Mike hurt your fingers?" asked Genesis as gently as possible.

"Yes," she said, and her eyes looked down in shame. "He said I was being too loud. He bent them until I heard them pop. And then I couldn't help but scream. Then he kicked me and stomped on me and then I must have fallen asleep," said Rachel.

"Where was your momma?" asked Genesis.

"She was at work. My grandma couldn't watch me that day. When that happens, Mike watches me. He's always mad and doesn't let me do anything," she said.

Genesis looked Rachel in the eyes and said solemnly, "Rachel, Jesus did make Mike. He made all people. But some people love Jesus, and some people don't love Jesus. The people who don't love Jesus do whatever they want, and sometimes they hurt other people. But Jesus sent me, so that you never have to be hurt by Mike again."

"I hope so. Momma said that he will never hurt me again, too," said Rachel.

"If you love Jesus, Rachel, He promises to never leave you or abandon you. He will even forgive you for all the bad things you have ever done, and He will only see the good in you," said Gen, "Do you believe that Rachel?"

"Yes, I do," Rachel said with a smile.

"Me, too," said Genesis and smiled back.

"I've got to go now and find your momma. I would like to talk to her too. And I have a few more kids I also need to talk to," said Gen.

"Will you come back later and tell me more about angels and Jesus?" asked Rachel.

"I will stop by again tomorrow. It was so nice to meet you, beloved," and Genesis winked and left the room.

After a very long first day, Genesis pulled her car to a stop in front of a small food and beer mart. Her apartment, or rather room, was just above it. She expected to see Lorenzo waiting in front to escort her to her room, but she remembered he had left town. She was pleasantly surprised to find Grant, smiling back at her.

"Hi. Sorry to disappoint you, but Lorenzo is off on his mission. So you just got me," he said sarcastically.

"Oh, that's right. Thanks for the flowers. They were beautiful," Genesis said looking at him.

"How was your birthday, Genesis?" asked Grant, warmly. "I was hoping to take you to dinner for your birthday and hear all about your first day."

She arched that one eye brown and studied him for a moment. "So, is this a debriefing or a date?" she asked.

"Definitely a date," he said with a wink. "If that's okay with you."

"Quite okay," responded Genesis, as she slid under his arm and they walked to his car.

CHAPTER 12

*The Lord is my strength and my shield; my heart
trusts in him, and he helps me.*
Psalm 28:7

Grant arrived just before eight and slipped into
his fatigues in the locker room. He was issued a sidearm and an AR-15. He remembered the powerful feeling that came with being armed: the alertness and the
adrenaline. He entered Major Arson's office and stood
at attention.

"Why aren't you chipped? It's been near impossible
to get you enlisted without a chip," Major Arson said
gruffly.

"I have a severe allergy to metals, Major Arson. When
they attempted to chip me, I nearly died. My body rejected the implant," responded Grant.

About three years ago, the entire world experienced
several deadly new strains of plagues. Millions of men,
women, and children died. The United Communist

Americas mandated that everyone be chipped in order to have quick access to medical information such as current vaccinations. The chip also monitored banking, since we went to a paperless money system, and government information such as crimes, taxes, and schooling. When Mexico, the United States, and Canada became one country, it allowed the government to stream line the change quickly. It really made life easier for everyone. But there were problems with the chips. There were some people who were allergic to the implants. There were some Christians and some Muslims who refused to be chipped. Some parents would not let their children be chipped until they were eighteen and could make their own decision. So, it was not a complete success yet, and the government was still pressuring every citizen to be chipped. If you weren't chipped, it made things like buying and selling, medical needs, and government transactions cumbersome. The unchipped people were often treated with contempt and ridiculed. They were the last people served, and the last people considered. It was humbling to say the least.

"You are quite the ninny for such a Goliath of a man," she quipped.

"I'm hardly Goliath," replied Grant, quietly.

Major Arson ignored his comment and handed him tickets. "You leave this afternoon. There is a situation in Louisiana. There is a work camp where there seems to be some sort of congregation going on. It needs to be broken up. I need names of the leaders and names of everyone who is a part of it. If there are people visiting the leaders from the outside, I want their names also. It is not a convenient time for me to travel. I will take actions based on your investigation. Call Private Neil, and he will book your return flight when you've completed your mission."

"And one more thing," she said as she handed him a file. "Here is all the information I have on this person, but I want more. I want to know everything. I think she is corrupt, and I want you to find corruption even if it's not there. Do you understand me?" She looked up at Grant to search his face for any sign of a conscience, a twitch or blink, but he simply stared straight ahead.

"Yes, Major Arson," Grant responded crisply.

"Good. Keep it confidential. Nothing goes through Private Neil. It all comes directly to me. That is all."

"Good day, Major Arson," said Grant and exited the office.

Grant stopped by Private Neil's desk on the way out. "So, how's the new job going, Neil?" asked Grant.

"Actually, not bad. My days fly by because she keeps me so busy. She has so many people coming and going from her office in a day. There's never a dull moment. But just between you and me, she is scary. You should watch your back. Better yet, I'll watch your back, and you watch my back. I just don't know if I can trust her," confided Neil.

Grant responded calmly, "A good man brings good things out of the good stored up in his heart, and an evil man brings evil things out of the evil stored up in his heart. For the mouth speaks what the heart is full of. This is how you will know whether you can trust Major Arson." Grant waved his plane ticket and said, "Thanks for arranging this. I'll be calling you in a few days for some tickets home. Take care." He smiled warmly at Neil and left.

With the new and dangerous position, Grant was very cautious driving back to the parking garage to make sure he wasn't followed, but he needed to inform Boxer and find out everything he could about the Christian operations in the south. The Partakers were predominantly a midwestern organization. It was difficult to communicate with other parts of the Americas because it is widely known that the Communist government monitors the web and cell phones. This would be a prime opportunity to share information with a southern Christian organization.

Grant and Boxer sat down on the worn brown couch and sipped coffee. Grant committed the names and phone numbers of the Christian leaders in Louisiana to memory. Then he took a few moments to hand write a note to Genesis to explain his absence and thank her for the wonderful evening the other night. Then he left for the airport.

The plane landed in Beaumont Municipal Airport late that evening. Grant picked up a rental car and drove to McDonald's at the Shell gas station on the corner. He ordered a cup of coffee and a large fry and sat down in a corner booth. A few minutes later, a gangly man in spectacles walked in and approached Grant. "I'm looking for my brother, Grant. Would that be you?"

Grant stood quickly and embraced the man warmly. "I certainly am. You must be Mark."

"Yes, I am, sir," responded Mark.

"I am eager to hear about all the work you are doing down here for the Kingdom Workers. And I have much to share with you from the Partakers," said Grant.

"First tell me why you are here. I must admit, I am surprised to see you in uniform. That must be quite a story," said Mark.

"Well, I entered the military when I was eighteen, back when we were still the United States. I was weeded out when the Communist Party took over the military. From there, I moved back with my father who was a preacher. He was under attack from the new local government for supposedly preaching hate and intolerance. As we saw the persecution grow, and churches burned or repurposed, and friends start to mysteriously die, disappear, or be sent to prison, my father and

I started the Partakers. An organized effort to rescue people who were to be imprisoned or terminated. We have rescued many but lost many also. We have people in the government, hospitals, schools, and prisons. I have worked as a civilian for the ACI, as a guard and as a teacher for several years. Recently, I was asked by Major Arson to enlist and work as a private investigator for her personally."

"Major Arson!" gasped Mark. "She has persecuted and imprisoned many of my fellow brothers and sisters. She has even ordered some to be executed. She is ruthless and evil. How do you intend to maintain your cover without compromising your soul?" asked Mark in wonder.

"Well, I might not be employed here very long. It's definitely the most dangerous position I've held. But I will be privy to intel that could save the lives of many Christians in the meantime. As you know, our God is faithful. My Jesus will supply all my needs."

"So, what brings you to Louisiana?" inquired Mark, squinting his nose to push his glasses back up.

"Major Arson wants me to investigate the congregation that is meeting inside the Beaumont Work Camp. I'm supposed to find out the names of the leaders, the followers, and anyone from the outside that meets with them," reported Grant.

Mark's face visibly whitened as he heard all of this. "Well, that's me. I smuggle in Bibles and things that they need. We call ourselves the Kingdom Workers. Your ministry is rescuing believers. Our ministry is to make believers and disciple them. There are many, many Muslims and criminals who have repented and accepted Jesus as their Lord and Savior. There are so many of us. Jesus has worked in miraculous ways, appearing in dreams and healing people. Even the hardest of hearts cannot deny what their eyes are seeing. It is very difficult to control the flow of information because the prisoners are so excited. They are telling everyone. Even the guards are getting saved. It is rumored that even the warden is looking the other way because he, himself, has become a believer. So, I can see how word of this might have gone all the way to Major Arson. What will we do?" asked Mark.

"What we always do. We will pray and fast and wait on the Lord. And He has already begun his work of deliverance because he sent you a believer to investigate you," Grant said encouragingly while placing his hand on top of Mark's hand.

CHAPTER 13

He causes his sun to rise on the evil and the good,
and sends rain on the righteous and the unrighteous.
Matthew 5:45

Darrell and Lorenzo's vans made it through another check point upon entering Thunder Bay. Shortly after the check point, they arrived at their first stop. Darrell and Lorenzo turned off their headlights and pulled in the long driveway to a nondescript house on a half-acre. Darrell activated the garage door and the two minivans pulled in side by side. Then he closed the doors behind them. They all piled out and entered the house that wasn't much bigger than the two-car garage. All the blinds were closed, and the house smelled musky. The house was completely empty except for the food and water piled high on the green, laminate kitchen counters. Darrell started giving directions.

"God has blessed our travels. We have here most of the food and water we will need during our travels. Bad news is it will be heavy. Good news is it gets lighter as we travel and eat," he said with a smile. A couple people chuckled softly at this. "This is our food for the next eight days until our next drop off point. Lorenzo is in charge of food, so he will show you how to pack it efficiently and ration it as we go," said Darrell. Darrell's dark skin glowed in the yellow light as he spoke.

"After you have packed your supplies, we will sleep here for the next six hours. Trevor, Autumn, and the baby will have the first bedroom. Trina, Devon, and Makayla will have the second bedroom. The rest of us will be out here. Any questions? Lights out in about an hour. But before you start packing your supplies, I just want to say how your faith and work has impressed me. I am honored to be traveling with you. You will be a great blessing and encouragement to the Panther's Refugee Camp. I love you guys," Darrell said genuinely as he looked at each person and smiled.

As Darrell laid on the hard floor in his army green sleeping bag, he rubbed his eyebrows, then rested his arm across his forehead, and went over tomorrow's foot journey in his mind. The Partakers have become family to Darrell. His father split when he was little. His mom was the rock of the family because she had to be. She always provided for him and his little sister and gave them a solid foundation in Jesus. Sadly, his mother lost a long battle with breast cancer when he was twenty.

He watched his little sister dissolve down to skin and bones in bondage to drugs after losing their mother. Seeing his sister's hopelessness drove him to the foot of the cross. He dropped out of medical school to care for his sister's needs. She eventually died from a drug overdose. At his lowest point, he met Grant, and he pointed him back to Jesus. Now he saw his path clearly ahead of him. His eyes were on Jesus.

The six hours of sleep passed too quickly. They got up while the moon was still in the sky. The two minivans of Panthers drove another hour and a half to the east side of Lake Nipigon. They arrived at another small house with a two-car garage. They pulled both minivans in side by side, shut the garage doors then exited the vehicles. Again, the house was completely empty, and the blinds were pulled. The small group of refugees walked through the house and out the back door into the dark cover of the woods, where their foot journey lay before them.

There was nearly 200 miles of hiking in front of them. If there were no problems, the goal was to hike through hundreds of miles of forest at a rate of twenty miles per day. They would arrive just north of the Fort Hope Indian Reserve in under two weeks. The Eabametoogn First Nation had known Boxer through some missionary work. He made life-long brothers there. The tribe had allowed them to secretly forge a small refugee camp north of their community. The Native Americans understood completely what it was like to be a foreigner in your own country. The tribe had lovingly taken the first Panthers and shown them how to retrieve water, grow crops, and build small homes and places for sewage. The natives warned these new settlers that the water in the area was poisoned from pollutants and had to boiled before being used. They shared with them the secrets of surviving through the harsh winters. The relationship between the two people groups was beautiful and God had blessed them both.

Darrell met Cheyenne Sugarhead, a member of the Eabatemoogn tribe, at the Panther Refugee Camp. He said it was her confidence in Christ alone, that drew him to her. She spoke unashamedly of what Jesus had done for her. But Cheyenne's tribe members tried to discourage her relationship with Darrell. Her family had been leaders in their tribe for many years. Some of the older population frowned on relationships with outsiders, for fear their heritage and race would not be preserved. But the Lord so clearly brought Darrell and Cheyenne together. As they worked side by side building the Panther's Refugee Camp their relationship continued to blossom.

Darrell led the group through fairly flat terrain most of the day. The rougher ground would start tomorrow. They ate breakfast while they walked and stopped for lunch. They had finished the twenty miles in time to set up camp for the night and make dinner.

After the easiest day of hiking, Darrell took a moment, to steal away by himself. He knew the days ahead would be more difficult. People would be tired, hungry, and irritable as they traveled in unfamiliar country with unfamiliar people. He went to his knees and spoke to His friend and Savior, Jesus. Breathing in the fresh air and looking at God's glorious creation, he thanked Jesus for their day's safe journey. He asked for wisdom to lead this great people. He prayed for Cheyenne's work with the Panthers. He prayed that they would care for her and love her in return for all she sacrificed for them. He prayed for their love and future together, God willing. Then, Darrell was ripped from his presence with Jesus by an unending scream that pierced his heart with fear. "No, no, no," he thought, as his strong legs pulsed towards the screaming.

CHAPTER 14

*The Lord is a refuge for the oppressed, a strong-
hold in times of trouble.*
Psalm 9:9

Genesis bent down to sit next to Miguel, a young
boy with golden skin and rich brown hair that swooped
down into his eyes. "How are you feeling today, Miguel?"

He peeked out from under his long bangs and
smiled at Genesis. "I feel fine. Just like I felt yesterday.
I don't even know why I'm here anymore," he said as he
bounced the ball up against the wall across from them.

Genesis recalled feeling the same way when she
was in the hospital just on the other side of the river-
bank. She recalled how close she was to disappearing
from this earth. She looked at Miguel with concern and
asked, "I notice you haven't been chipped yet. Why is
that?"

Miguel's countenance changed, and his voice became defensive. "You aren't chipped either. Besides a lot of kids my age aren't chipped yet. What's your excuse?"

"I'm a follower of Jesus Christ," she responded confidently.

"Huh! My mom and dad are too! They told me not to ever take the "mark," as they call it. I don't know. I've seen how hard life has gotten for them and how people treat them. If it gets worse, and I don't take the mark, who will take care of them?"

"Do your parents seem afraid about that?" asked Genesis.

"No," replied Miguel.

"I know why. They trust that Jesus will provide for them until it is time for them to leave this earth, and then He will carry them to heaven just as He promised."

"I don't know about all that. Do you believe all that?" asked Miguel.

Genesis glanced up and caught the eye of the play therapist and smiled. Genesis was unsure if the therapist could hear their conversation. Genesis replied to Miguel, "I believe it with my whole heart. And I would give my life to tell others about Jesus because the time will soon be here when He returns for His people. I want to know Miguel, that you will be with me when He comes for us," Genesis said gently. She waited a few moments then said, "Miguel, would you pray with me and trust Jesus to be your Savior?"

Miguel bounced the ball off the wall one more time. Then he looked straight ahead at the wall, deep in thought. "Yes, I will," said Miguel.

They closed their eyes and prayed together. That day the angels rejoiced. Genesis cried and embraced Miguel, and the play therapist watched carefully, taking in everything that was going on.

Just then, Miguel's parents walked in the room. "Mom, Dad!" He hugged them and whispered his exciting news into his parent's ears.

Juan and Maria, Miguel's parents, both stared in astonishment at Genesis. Genesis stood up and brushed off her black leggings and straightened her long waisted, wine blouse. She smiled at them, still uncertain of their reaction. Juan and Maria both quickly approached Genesis and hugged her graciously. There were tears and thank yous and more hugs. The play therapist leaned back in her chair and watched, apparently mystified by the whole interaction.

Genesis finally broke away and was able to ask them if they would join her in her office. She had some questions for them. The play therapist escorted Miguel back to his room, and Juan and Maria began to follow Genesis back to her office.

As they exited the elevator, Genesis saw Aarav with his mop. "Can you excuse me just a moment," Genesis said to Miguel's parents, and then walked over to Aarav.

"Aarav, how are you, my brother?" asked Genesis.

"Very good. All is well with my soul. What can I do for you, my child?" he asked in his thick accent from India.

"I need you to pray that God will give me wisdom. Plead for the life of Miguel and his family," said Genesis.

"Is that the family, over there?" asked Aarav.

"Yes. It is," replied Gen.

"I will go before our Father. He is ever present in our time of need," he replied.

"Thank you, Aarav," said Genesis and gave his arm a squeeze.

Once in her office, Genesis sat down to address Miguel's parents with her concerns, but Juan started the conversation first.

"I am concerned for the safety of my son," Juan said.

"I am as well," said Genesis, furrowing her brow. "Has Miguel ever had any issues with eating?"

"No. Just when he was sick this last week. We brought him into the ER because he had been running a fever and throwing up for three days," replied Maria.

"We were surprised when they admitted him. His doctor says he has a tumor in his stomach," said Juan. "We have asked to see the results of the MRI, but we haven't seen the doctor since then. We were just told by a resident that the surgery was scheduled for tomorrow morning. We have so many questions. Is it a benign tumor or cancerous? Will there be chemotherapy or radiation? And why are we talking to a social worker?" said Juan, clearly exasperated.

"We are so, so very thankful that Miguel has met you and prayed to have Jesus as the Lord of his life! But Miguel is our only child. This is all happening so fast. It seems so strange. Why aren't we getting clear answers from anyone? Do you think you can help us?" asked Maria, desperately.

"Can you answer some more questions for me, first?" asked Genesis. Both parents shook their heads yes. Maria crossed her feet and folded her hands trying to calm her nerves.

"Can you describe Miguel's eating habits before all of this happened?"

"Why?" asked Maria, defensively.

"Love, just answer the questions. She is for us, not against," said Juan reassuringly.

"He eats eggs and toast almost every morning for breakfast. He eats beans and rice for lunch or a meat sandwich if he is at school, with veggies or an apple, of course. I am a good mama," Maria added with a worried expression.

"I'm sure that you are, Maria. I have to have paperwork to support my recommendation," explained Genesis.

"For dinner we might eat out. It's just the three of us, you know. But sometimes, I will make soup or taquitos or tacos," said Maria.

"Do either of you ever take away meals from Miguel as a form of punishment?" Genesis asked gently, knowing that this question was going to offend them.

"No! My Miguel, he is a good boy! He listens, and he honors us," said Maria, clearly offended now.

Juan, lowered his head, then added, "There was one time that I found Miguel had left the mower outside overnight. He did not put it away like I've taught him to. The next morning, when I found the lawn mower, I was angry. I sent him to school without his breakfast."

"Was this the only time that happened?" asked Genesis.

"Yes," replied Juan.

"Have you noticed a change recently in Miguel's mood? Has he seemed angry or depressed?"

"No. He is a happy boy," replied Maria, and Juan shook his head in agreement.

Genesis set her pen down and lifted her head and said, "Okay, my social worker questions are done. Let's just talk for a few minutes as a family in the kingdom of God." Genesis looked from Maria to Juan. "I am very concerned as well for your son. Have you heard of Christians disappearing or dying without explanation?"

"Yes," replied Juan, solemnly. "All Christians must be aware of this by now. We all live in the hands of our Savior now. We have a close friend and a relative who are both gone. One never returned from a vacation, and another was a young healthy man who mysteriously died after a minor procedure."

"May I ask the name of the person who never returned from a vacation?" asked Genesis.

"It was my sister, Teresa, Teresa Garcia, but she loved Jesus. She is with Him now."

"I am so sorry," comforted Maria. "How old was she?"

"She was forty-two when she disappeared two years ago. She never married. She always said her Lord Jesus was more than enough to meet all of her needs," she replied.

"Can we please pray together?" asked Genesis.

"Of course," they both replied, and the three saints bowed their heads in unity and beseeched their God.

"Jesus, give me wisdom and protection as I speak with my brother and sister. Jesus, give them clear direction in the days to come. Amen."

"I want you to go home tonight and think and pray very carefully about what I'm going to say. I am afraid, Miguel has been marked for termination. These hospitals mark Christians for unnecessary procedures and then use their organs for other people. I know this is hard to hear, but because of your sister's disappearance, it is even more likely the case that this is what is happening. Please listen to me very carefully now. I would advise that you remove Miguel from the hospital as soon as possible. All you need to do is ask a nurse for an AMA form. It says you are removing your son against medical advice. That releases the hospital of all responsibility if anything happens to your son. They will then try to find me to see if I have any evidence of neglect. They won't be able to find me easily. When they do find me, I will slowly go over all my notes with them in which I will not find any evidence against you."

"What if they come to our home and try to take him from us?" Maria asked, in a near panic.

"Most likely they will come to your home because you're denying your son a lifesaving surgery. So, you will have to go into hiding. Not for a week or a month, but for the rest of your lives. Please do not make this decision lightly but do make it quickly and prayerfully. If you decide to go into hiding, my group can provide a safe place for you to hide. Just come this evening with one piece of luggage each to this address and wait in the parking garage until a believer approaches you." Then Genesis rose from her chair and handed Juan a piece of paper with the address on it. "Please completely destroy that paper. I and many others will be praying for your family." She embraced them both and walked them to the elevator.

"I will see you again someday. Goodbye," she said to Maria and Juan.

"Goodbye and thank you. We will never forget what you have done for us, and what you have risked by doing so," said Juan.

CHAPTER 15

Because the hand of the Lord my God was on me,
I took courage and gathered leaders from Israel to
go up with me.
Ezra 7:28

The next morning, Grant drove to the entrance of the Venice, Louisiana's work camp #07. He slowed to a stop at the guard shack and showed his ID. The man in fatigues waved him through the high security, fenced in facility. Grant got out of the car and scoped out the environment. It was a two-story brown brick building. There were large windows towards the front of the building but only small twelve by twelve-inch windows for as far back as he could see. There was a black awning at the entrance. To the right of the building were multiple large garage doors where semis could load and unload. There were guards posted at the front of the building and at every entrance. There appeared to be a yard to the right with a scattering of grey wooden picnic tables.

Grant left his AR-15 in the trunk and just kept his sidearm on him. He saluted the military guards at the entrance and walked to the central desk to check in.

"I have an appointment at eight with Warden Ledbetter. I am Officer Grant Panther from ACI in Minneapolis," said Grant.

"You're a long way from home, Officer," said the private behind the desk. "Have a seat over by the window, and someone will come get you shortly."

No sooner had Grant sat down, when another officer called his name. He followed the other officer to an office just a few steps away.

Kendall Ledbetter shook hands with Grant at the entrance to his office. Then said, "Please, have a seat, Officer Panther. What brings you all the way to Louisiana?" asked Kendall in his Louisiana twang.

"Please, call me Grant," he said as he shifted in his chair to get comfortable. Kendall was an older man, probably in his early sixties. His head was shiny and bald. He had on dark blue slacks with a plaid short sleeve shirt. Grant noticed a cowboy hat on the table near his desk.

"Major Arson sent me here to check on a religious congregation that she has been getting reports of. She was unable to make it here herself. Do you know who could've made this complaint?" asked Grant.

"Didn't Major Arson give that information to you?" asked Kendall, who was already showing signs of being defensive.

"No, she didn't. I had to leave rather quickly. Are you aware of any groups of people meeting for religious purposes?" asked Grant.

"There are four to five men per room, building and packaging cellular phones from 8 a.m. until 8 p.m., so if you call that congregating, yes they congregate. Is it religious? I have no idea what their conversations are about over those twelve hours of work. There are over four hundred men working here. Let me walk you around our facility, so you can better understand what I'm talking about," said Kendall as he pushed back from his chair and stood up.

Grant stood as well. As they walked Grant asked, "Do you like working here, Kendall?"

"Why? Is my job in danger?" asked Kendall, looking out the corner of his eye at Grant, suspiciously.

"No. It was just a general question. So, do you like running this place?" asked Grant again.

"Ya know, Grant. Three years ago, I would have said no, and I would've welcomed retirement, demotion, or anything other than coming here every day. But things are different now. As you'll see. The place hums. These men are in the lowest position you could put them in life, and yet they seem content somehow. I don't exactly understand it myself, but the environment has changed," replied Kendall as he opened a door for Grant into a monotone hallway.

The facility was divided into four long hallways. The first two hallways they walked down were living quarters. There were cells on the right, and cells on the left. Two stories of them. Two bunks per cell. The grey tile floors echoed as the two men walked down the halls.

"Three years ago, we had at least three fights a day, and at least one knifing a week. There is so much equipment and various tools laying around, it was almost impossible to protect the men from each other. And then on top of that, they had to work together and produce a functioning phone. It was a nightmare. I hated coming to work. I felt like a failure every day when I left. Even tried praying. Bargaining with God. If anyone could've shown me how to run this pit of hell, I would've done anything they asked," he chuckled to himself and rubbed his head again.

Grant looked at him graciously, "So what changed?"

"Well, we got some leadership. And it wasn't even me! There was this worker, Stephen. He just turned everything around. The guys listened to him and respected him. He organized everything. Got everything cleaned up and running like a top. I've never had it so easy," said Kendall shaking his head.

"I would have given him anything he wanted to just keep it up, but he's not like other people. Most men here would demand special hours, special quarters, cigarettes, or female visitors. This guy never asked for anything. And when I offered him anything, just out of appreciation, he wouldn't even accept it. I don't get what makes this guy tick, but he's been great for this facility and my career. I'm surprised they even listened to a complaint from here because we outperform every other facility," said Kendall.

"So, do you think Stephen is our leader of the congregation?" asked Grant.

"I'll let you decide that. But y'all are nuts to do anything to jeopardize what we've got going on here," said Kendall honestly. "These last two halls are the work areas," said Kendall as he opened the door for Grant. "As you can see, it has the same set up as the first two hallways except four to five men are in each cell." Grant looked around as Kendall continued talking. The men all wore the same white jumpsuits. They all appeared clean shaven and pleasant. The guards were dressed in black. Most of them were walking the halls and occasionally chatting with some of the workers. Grant even watched one of the guards on the floor helping one of the workers look for a small part that rolled away. Some were working on the floors and some were working on the bunks, assembling minuscule parts on cells phones. As they walked, Grant overheard some humming here and there. He thought he recognized one of the tunes. Others were talking quietly about family members and politics. He was sure he heard scripture references a couple of times. Runners would run the phones from one cell to the next in an assembly line. The final runner would leave the hallways and run the finished product, cleaned, packaged, and boxed, to the garage where there were docks to load the boxes. There was also a dock for unloading. A team of men unloaded boxes and parts, and then runners distributed them.

"This is a pretty amazing facility. It's hard to believe this is a work camp. It's hard to believe these aren't paid men working here. An impressive, fine-tuned operation," said Grant, genuinely.

"Let me introduce you to Stephen," said Kendall. They walked toward a man about Grant's age and height but built like a farm boy. He moved with confidence and strength. He had short hair that was a blazing orange and crystal blue eyes. When he saw the men approaching, he paused what he was doing and addressed the warden respectfully.

"Good morning, Warden Ledbetter," he said warmly, and when he smiled, his large ears moved up slightly on his head.

"Good morning, Stephen," said Kendall, "I would like you to meet Officer Grant from the ACI in Minneapolis. He would like to ask you a couple of questions. I would like you to listen to him and answer his questions carefully."

Stephen turned towards Grant and gave him his full attention. "How can I help you, Officer Grant?" He paused and looked intently for a moment at Grant then he said, "I'm sorry, but do I know you from somewhere?"

Grant could see the strength of God's grace resting on this man. He saw the familiar joy of his face that Grant so often had to hide on his jobs. It was all Grant could do to stop himself from embracing the man in brotherly love. "No, I don't think you do," said Grant.

Grant looked him in the eye and said, "So, Stephen, we have received word that there is a religious congregation meeting here regularly. I'm here to investigate the leader and any of the participants in this religious congregation. Are you aware of any such happenings or leader?" asked Grant.

If Stephen's warm smile could've gotten any wider, it did, just then. "Why yes! I'm the leader. There are many of us. We are followers of Jesus Christ. We call ourselves the Kingdom Workers. We meet daily at lunch, and I preach. I preach again on Sundays, our day off. Each cell has a group leader that leads them in worship and Bible study in the mornings while they are building. If it's alright with Warden Ledbetter, I would love to have you join us at lunch for the teaching."

Both Stephen and Grant looked over to Warden Ledbetter, who was looking at his shoes, shaking his head in disbelief at what Stephen had just confessed to. Ledbetter rubbed his shiny head like a man rubbing a genie bottle, wishing that this just didn't happen. Finally, Ledbetter said, "sure, why don't you join them for lunch. Grant, why don't we walk back to my office and talk before lunch," suggested Ledbetter.

Grant obliged and shook Stephen's hand and thanked him for answering his questions before the men left.

Grant prayed as he walked silently beside Kendall back to the office. He knew what God was asking him to do.

Kendall shut the door after they entered the office. As Kendall walked to his desk, he began, "Now, Officer Grant ..."

Grant interrupted, "I, too, am a follower of Jesus Christ."

"Whaaaat?" responded Kendall in total confusion. Kendall sat there in disbelief, letting all the ramifications of that statement sink in. "How is that possible? You work for ACI? Aren't you here to investigate an Int crime? Is Major Arson aware of this?"

"No. She is not. I would greatly appreciate if it stayed that way. My life would be in great danger if she found out."

"You Jesus people are everywhere. It's like I couldn't hide from God if I tried!" Kendall said, exasperated.

"Can you give me more insight as to what has been going on in this facility over the last few years?" asked Grant.

"Well, I've never seen anything like it in all my years. Stephen came here, and it started with the cell he was in. His attitude, or whatever it was, was like the only light in this whole pit of darkness. Then the guys he worked with slowly started changing. I began to get complaints about him singing and teaching all the time. I didn't care. It was four less people trying to kill each other."

Kendall continued. "The guards use to facilitate the work, and they sucked at it. Well, Stephen would make suggestions, and they worked. The guards started going to him with questions. Before you knew it, he was working into the wee hours with the guards and the other three guys from his cell to set things up to run more efficiently. He also put his three buddies in other cells as leaders. Before I knew it, there were sixteen of these Jesus people and three guards! But then some really weird stuff started happening. The leaders of some of the hardest guys in here started having dreams. Some of them were terrifying, some of them saw angels, and one Muslim guy said he saw Jesus himself in his dream! There was so much commotion, I think even Stephen was taken aback. The only thing Stephen could think to do was to start teaching during lunches, to help the workers understand what was happening to them, according to the scriptures."

"Then one day, everything changed. There was a fight during lunch out on the grounds. Two guys were fighting. It was a bad one. Everyone crowded around, and my guards couldn't get to them. Lenny had twisted Marcel's arm behind him. Then with one stomp, he broke Marcel's arm. There was a shriek of pain that sent me and the remaining guards running in that direction. Then Lenny pulled out a knife and stabbed him in the back!"

"I heard Stephen yell, 'Let me through.' The men respected Stephen. They let him through. Stephen fell to his knees next to Marcel. He cried out loud to Jesus. He asked for Jesus to heal him. Stephen placed his hand on Marcel's torn shirt and bloody back and bowed his head and wept. When Stephen lifted his hand, the hole was gone. The hole where the knife went in was gone! Then Stephen went to his arm. We all could heard the snap when Lenny broke it. We saw the strange, unnatural angle it had laid at his side. But when Stephen wrapped his hands around his arm it began to straighten out. Stephen then helped Marcel up. Lenny had dropped to his knees and was repenting! Workers and guards began praising God side by side. We've never been the same since. I couldn't have stopped it if I had tried. It wasn't from this earth!" said Kendall, looking wildly at Grant for answers.

"Kendall, do you believe in Jesus now?" asked Grant.

"I would have to deny what I saw with my own eyes to deny Him. Yes, I do," replied Kendall.

"Do you believe that you are a sinner, and you need Jesus' forgiveness?" asked Grant.

At these words, Kendall broke down in tears and covered his face with his hands. "I've done it all wrong. I ran this place all wrong for years. I hurt so many people, God's people. How could He ever forgive me?"

Grant responded gently, "Jesus has already covered the debt for all your sins, Kendall. If you trust Him, He will forgive all your sins. He loves you so much that He died for all that you've done wrong. He paid the price so you wouldn't have to, and so He could spend eternity with you. Would you like to pray and receive this gift Jesus has for you?" asked Grant.

"Yes, yes. I need him so badly," said Kendall.

And there, in that office, at a communist work camp, the warden prayed with Grant and asked Jesus to be the Lord of his life and the work camp.

CHAPTER 16

He rescues and he saves; he performs signs and
wonders in the heavens and on the earth. He has
rescued Daniel from the power of the lions.
Daniel 6:27

Darrell's heart was racing. The woman's scream was getting closer as he raced through camp and to the west side. He saw in the clearing Lorenzo holding back Matthew from the edge of a cliff. Then he saw Paul standing over his mother as she cowered there screaming. Luke stood back from the group, holding Judah close to his side. Both boys stared ahead in shock.

Devon came running to meet Darrell. Devon said, "The boys wandered off, and Peter fell off the cliff."

"No," whispered Darrell. Darrell pushed passed Devon to the edge of the cliff. He saw Peter's motionless body. His legs were plastered unnaturally against the unforgiving earth beneath him, and his arm was under his body. It was so far down. The drop was at least fifty feet. He spun around and raced to find a way down the cliff. This was off their path, so Darrell was unfamiliar with the terrain. Frantically, he slid down the side of the embankment. Devon, Trevor, and Matthew were right behind him. Darrell began to slide so fast that his body began to roll, and then he finally hit the bottom. His head bounced off a rock. Devon landed painfully on Darrell's legs. Trevor and Matthew's fall was a bit more controlled. Darrell was up and running towards Peter. The rocks beneath him slid as he rushed to Peter's side.

Darrell's hand frantically looked for a pulse on the thirteen-year-old's neck, then on his wrist. He noticed a large cut on the back of Peter's head where blood was beginning to pool. Then Darrell noticed Peter's blue eyes staring straight ahead. Darrell's dusty hand went unconsciously to the boy's eye lids and lovingly closed them. Then with everything within him, from the depths of his soul poured the name, "Jeeeeeeeeeeeeeeeeeesus. Help me! Bring him back, Jeeeeeeeesus."

Lorenzo appeared finally among the men. He bent carefully and double checked for a pulse. "Let's pray. The mighty men of this group lifted their voices to their God. They pleaded for mercy to bring the boy back. It continued on until the women and children joined them at the base of the cliff. They all gathered around, crying, begging, bargaining, and finally surrendering. Night fall came, and the group didn't move. They cried and prayed and sang until the sun lit the horizon above the trees.

Everyone knew what needed to be done, but no one wanted to begin the final goodbyes. Darrell's voice broke the silence, hoarse from the night's prayers. "Matthew and Ashley, you need to decide your next step. We can pull Peter on a sled back the twenty miles to the home in Nipigon, or we can bury Peter here and continue on our way to the refugee camp. The decision is yours. The rest of us are going to go back to the top of the cliff, to our camp. Please, come get us when you make your decision. I am so, so very sorry." Darrell dropped his head and began to walk back to the embankment where he had slid down. The others followed, helping one another up the steep slope. Matthew, Ashley, and their children held each other in a tight circle and spoke in hushed tones.

An hour later, the family returned to the camp. Everyone sat up and greeted them. Matthew spoke for the family. "We have decided to bury Peter here and continue on to the refugee camp. This has been a very difficult decision. But when we thought of what Peter would have wanted, it was clear to us. He loved God's creation. He has always been adventurous. It was his enthusiasm that carried the family through the uncertainties about going to the refugee camp." Matthew's voice began to break. "We found a very small pond at the bottom of the hill that Peter would have loved to fish in the early morning hours. We would like to bury him there and build some sort of memorial or marker for him." One by one, each person got up and embraced this hurting family. Together they would make it through this trial and trust Jesus for tomorrow.

The following day, the somber group began once again their long journey to the Fort Hope Indian Reserve. Darrell led them. Lorenzo followed at the rear. They chatted in groups of twos and threes as they walked mile after mile. After the twentieth mile, Darrell stopped and announced that this would be their resting point for the night. The group collapsed in the midst of the woods by a strange pillar of rocks. The men and the women began to gather sticks and rocks to build a fire for their well-deserved evening meal.

While the group was eating, Darrell began to tell them about the strange pillar of rocks to the left of their camp site. "It was my third trip when I watched Grant build that pillar of rocks. He was the lead, and I brought up the back. We were camped out here. We had twelve refugees just like now. We had the group take turns, just like we will tonight, to stay up and keep watch. The fire ambers were still burning. It was Grant's shift, around

1a.m., when he heard the slight snap of a branch. He turned behind him and saw some movement in the darkness. Then Grant heard another sound in a different direction, and it was deep and ominous. Then Grant saw them. Three full grown, black bears, coming from three directions walking on all fours towards Grant's group. They were a mere two feet away from the campers soundly sleeping in their sleeping bags. I must have sensed something because I awoke and saw Grant's eyes wide and staring into the darkness. I saw the three bears approaching, but before I could calculate what we could do, the bears were on the campers. Grant stood straight up. His eyes were not on the bears, but up where his help would come from. And Grant cried out to the heavens, in a guttural sound, 'Faaaaaaatther!' Then he paused, and he listened for his Father's answer. A moment later, Grant clapped his hands together with such might that my ears were ringing. Then he shouted, 'Go! In the name of Jesus!' with such force that I flinched. The bears turned and ran back into the forest. By then, all the group was awake. We all broke out in prayer and praise. God had rescued us! That morning, Grant built that pillar of rocks to remind him and everyone who passes through here that God is the one who rescues us in our time of need."

Darrell's head dropped in sorrow. He paused to collect himself then said, "It may not seem as though God rescued Peter. But we know from this pillar that God is always with us. He may not have rescued Peter from his fall, but He rescued him from his sin, and he is in Paradise with Jesus this day."

"Thank you," said Matthew. Then the group began one by one to snuggle down for the night, and the fire began to burn low as Lissa began to cough and fuss. "I'll stay up for the first watch, since Lissa is fussy anyway," said Trevor.

"I'll take second shift," said Lorenzo. "Wake me up at one."

"I'll do third," said Devon. "Wake me up at three."

"I will do a devotional at six, and then we will head out," said Darrell. "Good night." Everyone echoed their goodnights.

But no one got much sleep that night. Lissa continued to cough and fuss. She was burning up with a fever by morning.

CHAPTER 17

But our citizenship is in heaven. And we eagerly
await a Savior from there, the Lord Jesus Christ.
Philippians 3:20

Genesis prayed as she walked toward the play therapy room. "Jesus, my relationship with Breelyn has been awkward. I don't know how to approach her, and she has sent signals not to approach her. But I like her. I love how she loves on the children. I want her to know You, Jesus, like I know You. Lord, help me to find favor in her eyes. Help me, Lord, to be genuine and loving the way You were with people. But, Lord, make me wise as a serpent and as gentle as a dove because these are perilous times. But don't ever let me forsake Your good news to protect myself and don't ever let my love grow cold."

Genesis smiled as she watched Breelyn on the floor interacting with a five-year-old who had both arms in casts. Breelyn was playing a game with the boy, using their feet. It was quite silly. They were both enjoying it. She noticed Genesis standing there watching, and Breelyn's expression completely changed.

"Hi, Genesis. Did you need to see someone?" asked Breelyn flatly.

"I was just going to grab lunch in the cafeteria, and I wanted to see if you wanted to join me. I can wait until you're done," said Gen with a smile.

Breelyn looked down at the young boy and said, "You win again, Dylan! It's time to go back to your room. I'll walk you there." Then she looked back at Gen and said, "That sounds great. I'll be right back."

Gen mouthed, "Thank you, Jesus," as Breelyn turned to walk Dylan back to his room. Breelyn was in her forties. She was married but didn't have any children. She wore her hair super short. She was a stunning African-American woman, and her short haircut displayed her wide set, tilted eyes, high cheek bones, and beautiful smile. She was confident to a fault, or at least that was the vibe she sent out.

Breelyn came wondering past Genesis without so much as a look and grabbed her purse behind her desk. "Let's go, hon," she said as she led the way to the cafeteria. Gen couldn't help but smile and hustled to catch up with her.

After moseying through the cafeteria line, Breelyn chose a seat by the window overlooking the Mississippi

River. Genesis sat down across from her and said, "Can I bless the food for us quickly?"

"Are you kidding me, girl? Uh-ah. You trying to get me fired? You go ahead and bless that lettuce. I'm going to be wild and just eat it cursed," said Breelyn with her eyebrows raised. Genesis chuckled, then bowed her head silently and thanked Jesus for her salad and Breelyn.

"Now don't go getting sensitive on me, Genesis," reprimanded Breelyn.

"Please, call me Gen. All my friends do," interrupted Gen.

"Gen, I haven't had anyone ask me to go to lunch, and I've been working here for four years. So, don't get offended that I'm not praying with you out here in public. But we can go to lunch together."

Genesis replied, "I totally understand."

They talked like good friends over lunch. And enjoyed learning about each other. Genesis was sad that there were parts of her life that she just couldn't share with Breelyn. She asked Breelyn, "I noticed that you aren't chipped. Why not?"

"I am married to a Muslim man. His name is Rafiq. He has forbidden me to be chipped. He believes it is from the devil and the devil's people."

Genesis asked, "So you are not Muslim?"

"No. I was raised here in the United States of America. My husband was raised in Yemen. Or what use to be Yemen in this crazy world," she said with a swipe of her hand at the air as though dismissing all the craziness. "I was raised in a devout Christian home. I was pretty much ostracized when I married a Muslim man. I renounced Jesus at that point. They just couldn't love me the way that I was. I'm not interested in people like that. Let that be a warning," she said as she glanced from her salad to Genesis.

"Duly warned," replied Gen with a wink.

"My turn to ask a question. What's the mark on your face and your hand?" asked Breelyn, almost tenderly.

Genesis self-consciously touched her cheek, and she felt the Holy Spirit nudge her to share. "I guess I need to work on my make-up. I thought I had perfected covering it up. I was burned down the entire right side of my body when I was a young girl. It was during the gassings in Minneapolis. Do you remember?" she asked Breelyn.

"Oh, my gosh, child. I am so sorry. I've never met anyone that was effected by that," replied Breelyn.

"That's because nearly all the families died because the fires happened at night when they were asleep. I was coming home from a friend's house late. When I opened the screen door, they think it might have made a static electric spark that set it off," Gen looked down at her hand and noticed she was covering her burned hand.

"Did you lose your whole family that night?" gasped Breelyn.

Genesis nodded her head yes. Then glanced at the powerful river outside the window.

"Now, what kind of a good God would take a child's family like that? Why wouldn't he stop such a terrible act?" asked Breelyn indignantly.

Genesis laid her scarred hand on the table in a pleading gesture. "Oh, it wasn't God who did that to my family. It was unbelievers. In fact, God even warned us that in the last days, things like this were going to happen. But he promised us that he would return to get us. He told us, during this time, many will fall away. Many will lose hope. But we must not lose hope. We must stay faithful to the end because we are not living for this world. We are like foreigners here. This is not our home. Our home is in heaven, where we will spend eternity. So our death here is inconsequential. My family lived for eternal life in heaven, and they have received it now."

"Well, I am terribly sorry you had to go through that. We better get back to work, or I'll be here until seven o'clock seeing all these kids," said Breelyn.

"I enjoyed sharing lunch with you, Breelyn. I'll find you tomorrow," said Genesis.

"Suit yourself. You know where to find me," replied Breelyn as she walked away.

CHAPTER 18

Be very careful, then, how you live-not as unwise
but as wise, making the most of every opportunity,
because the days are evil.
Ephesians 5:15-16

Grant followed the waitress at Denny's to a table near the kitchen. She started to place the menus on the table.

"Do you think I could have that large booth over there in the corner, please?" asked Grant politely.

"Sure," responded the waitress. She placed four menus down on the other table. "Your waiter will be right with you." Then, without a glance, she walked back to her podium at the front of the restaurant.

Mark arrived first. Grant waved him over and wondered at how he ever found pants that were that long and that small waisted. "Thanks for coming, Mark," he said, and he stood and shook his hand warmly.

"I wouldn't miss this for the world," said Mark. "I didn't sleep a wink last night. Who else is coming?"

Grant smiled at Mark and said, "I think you know him." With a wave of his hand, Grant motioned for Stephen. Mark turned and saw Stephen, the leader of the movement taking place inside Work Camp #07, walking towards him, free and without his white jump suit.

"What?" Mark exclaimed in shock as he saw the man with fire red hair cross the restaurant towards them. Mark stood up and embraced Stephen. "Are you free?" asked Mark.

"Yes! Of course, since the day I met our Savior. Those walls mean nothing to me," said Stephen. "But your faithfulness and brotherly love has meant so much to me," said Stephen, then he clasped hands with Grant. "Thanks for springing me, my new brother," he said with a huge smile.

"I just can't believe you're sitting here with us, Stephen," said Mark again as he pushed his glasses back up his nose with his finger.

"Then you really aren't going to believe our next companion for the evening," said Grant. Grant smiled as he saw the older cowboy walk in the door of Denny's and remove his hat. He looked around and saw Grant wave him over.

"Warden Ledbetter. What is he doing here? I think I'm going to need a scotch, and I don't even drink!" said Mark in total disbelief.

Grant formally introduced them. "Mark, this is your new brother in Christ, Warden Kendall Ledbetter. This is Mark. He has been the leader on the outside that has supplied all the needs for the Kingdom Workers I've been telling you about."

Kendall put out his hand and gave Mark a good strong shake. "I'm going to need some background story here," said Mark.

So, Grant began to tell how these four godly men were all divinely brought together.

"So, what's the next step?" asked Stephen, clearly excited. "Why do you think God has brought all of us together?"

Grant cleared his voice. "I haven't had the amount of time in prayer about this that I would like to have had. I need to get back to Minneapolis tomorrow. So, let's cover this conversation with prayer now."

All four men bowed their heads, "Dear Jesus, please, Lord, guide our steps as we move forward on our humanly time frame. Give us clear indication of what your will is for us. Bless our relationship, and may it bring glory to Your kingdom." Deep amens rumbled across Denny's and several customers looked in their direction.

Grant began again. "I know one purpose was to reassure Major Arson that the rogue church meetings down here are of no concern. It is run by a zealot that most workers find annoying at the least, but more than likely, he is crazy. The driven warden has the people working from the moment the sun rises until they drop into bed. They are too tired to pursue anything else.

"The other purpose I see is to improve our communication up north. The only form of communication the Partakers up north have that is safe are handwritten notes. Many times, people's lives hang in the balance, and time is of the essence. So, Kendall and Stephen are making us a hundred phones that are clean; no GPS or bugging mechanisms.

"Yet another reason for our divine meeting is to get Bibles in the hands of the young believers at this facility so that they can be discipled. Mark, can you get ahold of four hundred Bibles?"

"Yes, it will take time and money, but I can arrange that. What a miracle! I can't believe I am living to see this! Praise God!" said Mark.

"I can get the Bibles to the boys without a problem," said Kendall.

"And I can get an effective discipleship program going. These men have been taking my word for truth. Now they will read the truth for themselves," said Stephen.

"The final purpose that I can see is that we will be a resource; a help in time of need for one another. The days are not going to get any easier from here on out. The birth pains and persecution are going to become harder. We will lose loved ones. Some of us here will die, for the name of Jesus. But we will rise again and live for all eternity. And we will see each other on the other side."

"Glory be to Him!" Stephen responded.

"Amen," said Mark.

The men then continued to work out the details together for future meetings and phone calls and deliveries. They were filled with hope and encouraged by one another's love and faith.

CHAPTER 19

*And no wonder, for Satan himself masquerades as
an angel of light.*
2 Corinthians 11:14

The Panthers were in trouble already, and they had hundreds of miles ahead of them. The third day of the journey was filled with rock-covered hills, and the sun was merciless on their necks. At the end of the first day, they had lost Peter. The thirteen-year-old boy fell to his death while out exploring with his brother Paul. The parents, Matthew and Ashley and their three remaining boys, Judah, Luke and Paul, were still mourning the loss. It was difficult for the whole group to leave that morning, knowing that Peter was being left behind. They stopped more frequently than normal as Peter's family broke down in tears, so overtaken by their loss. And no one could ignore the moaning of little Lissa as she rode precariously on her father's back as she burned with fever and coughed painfully. The morale of the group was very low, and doubt and indecision became palpable. Ten miles into the hike, they came to a small stream. Autumn asked if they could stop and bathe Lissa in the stream in hopes of bringing her fever down a bit. Darrell, of course, agreed and asked if he could do anything to help. But there was little anyone could do in the middle of the wild forests of Canada.

Darrell put Lorenzo in charge and went to scout the area out. He left marks on trees as he went and kept his compass out so as not to get lost. About a mile west of the stream where he left the group, Darrell found a small log homestead. There was a water tank perched on top of the small flat roof, a miniature vegetable and herb garden out back. Chickens roamed freely around the house, and a goat was chained to a post out front. Darrell was greeted by a barking Blue Heeler that kept him from getting any closer. A woman came out of the front door with a rifle pointed at Darrell.

"What the devil brings you to my doorstep, way out here, ay?" demanded the woman in a fearless voice. Her shoulder length brown hair was matted down with sweat around the edges. Her jeans were torn at the knees and stained brown from gardening. The rifle rested comfortably on her oversized white, man's undershirt.

Darrell raised his hands and spoke in an unthreatening tone. "I am out hiking and camping with two of my friends. They have a three-month-old baby that is sick. She is coughing and burning up with fever. I need to get the baby out of the elements and find her some help."

"What's the baby's name?" asked the woman.

"Lissa. Her parent's names are Trevor and Autumn. Do you know where I can get help for them?" Darrell asked earnestly.

"I'm a nurse. Bring them here, and I'll see what I can do," said the nurse.

"They are a mile east of here by the stream. They are bathing the baby in the stream to try and bring the fever down. It will take about an hour to get them back here. Thank you so much for helping. They will be so relieved," said Darrell gratefully.

"Tell them to get that baby out of the stream. The water round here is all tainted. I wouldn't even bathe in it without boiling it first. I'll get some water boiling and some towels," she said as she put the rifle down.

"Thank you, again. I'll tell them and bring them back," said Darrell with a wave. Then he turned and began to run back towards the stream.

About an hour later, Darrell, Trevor, Autumn, and little Lissa were greeted by the barking dog. The woman walked out and shooed the dog away. She smiled warmly at Autumn and Lissa. "Can I hold her?" she asked Autumn kindly. Autumn handed her the swaddled baby.

"Let's get out of the sun. My name is Barbara. I've never had this many people in my home at one time. I hope we all fit," she said, chuckling to herself.

Barbara cooed and fussed over the baby. She took her temperature and undressed her right on her small, wooden kitchen table. Then she gave her some liquid ibuprofen out of a dropper. She expertly wrapped Lissa in some cool, wet towels and then rubbed some lavender, that probably came from her garden, on the baby's tiny feet. The baby seemed grateful for the attention and showed signs of life for the first time in twenty-four hours. Then Barbara transferred Lissa to a pillow on the floor. Autumn, Trevor, and Darrell watched in amazement as she cared for the baby.

"Now, we will just wait and see how she does in the next twenty-four hours, ay? I've only got one chair and one bed, so you'll have to make yourselves comfortable on the floor. I don't have any phone or electricity out here, and I don't have a car. Every Sunday, my son comes to bring me food and checks to see how I'm doing. So, I'm all ya got right now," said Barbara.

Autumn said genuinely, "You're an angel as far as I'm concerned. An answer to my prayers. I'm so thankful we found you! God is so good! He even brought us a nurse! How long did you work as a nurse?"

Darrell rubbed the back of his neck. Something was bothering him. Something Autumn said: "an angel."

Then Darrell remembered, "The enemy will appear as an angel of light."

"About fifteen years, at the Children's Hospital at UMMC in Minneapolis."

"That's the area we are from," said Autumn.

"Oh, ya don't say," said Barbara. "Gosh, I miss the children, but I don't miss the parents. No offense, but there are mighty bad parents out there. Some have no business parenting! I could fix the kids, but I couldn't fix the parents, and then I'd have to send the kids home with them. I felt so helpless. Well, I just said, 'enough of this,' and here I am. I've had enough of the world and these people. Oh, listen to me on my soap box," rambled Barbara. "I've got two Coca-Cola bottles my son brought me. They're warm, but would you like to share them?" she asked pleasantly.

Trevor and Autumn answered at the same time, "Sure!"

Darrell just sat on the floor quietly looking at Lissa, sleeping peacefully for the first time. He should've been thankful, even happy, but instead he was filled with foreboding.

CHAPTER 20

So I reflected on all of this and concluded that the
righteous and the wise and what they do are in
God's hands, but no one knows whether love or
hate awaits them.
Ecclesiastes 9:1

Dianne sat down at Chili's and greeted her friend Gretchen Rueport. Dianne was the HR director at the East Bank Hospital, and Gretchen was the HR director at Children's Hospital. The waitress approached, smiling. Her whole face shimmered with piercings in her nose, ears, lips, tongue, and even her cheek. "My name is Ty. Can I get you anything to drink?"

"Diet Coke," said Dianne.

"Margarita," said Gretchen. "Oh, and we have one other person we are waiting on."

"Okay," said Ty and hurried away to place the drink order.

"Oh, there's Cindy," said Gretchen as she waved her over.

"You know her, don't you? Doctor Houston's nurse," asked Gretchen. Dianne noticed Gretchen's red curls were especially tight and bouncy tonight, and it made her smile to herself.

"I only know of her. She was hired in long before I worked there, and I'm almost never on her floor so our paths don't really cross. But it will be nice to get to know her," said Dianne.

"Hi, Cindy!" said Gretchen. "This is Dianne. Dianne this is Cindy." Dianne smiled warmly at her then tucked here dark hair behind her ears nervously.

"You look a wreck! Did you have a bad day?" inquired Gretchen in a playful but caring way.

Ty returned with the drinks. "Can I get you anything to drink?" asked Ty, while she scanned the room and her other tables.

"I'll take a beer. Whatever you have on tap," replied Cindy. Then she turned to Dianne and said, "I've seen you around. How are you doing?"

"Good, thanks!" said Dianne.

"Why do you look so frazzled?" asked Gretchen.

"Well, Chris, that's Dr. Houston," said Cindy to Dianne and then she continued, "wanted to, you know, see me tonight. And I told him no. I'm not going to keep sharing him with his wife. He told me he was going to leave her, but I'm afraid it's just all talk with him. He keeps saying it will wreck the kids. But nowadays, kids understand. This stuff happens all the time."

"So, are you going to stop seeing him?" asked Gretchen, while Dianne uncomfortably sipped on her Diet Coke and looked around the room.

Cindy flashed her long thick eyelashes at Gretchen and then at Dianne and said, completely exasperated, "Oh, of course not! Have you seen the man, Dianne? He is just hot! And he is a genius, and he's saving the world. Does it get any better than that?" Cindy said in almost a squeal as she flung her thick beautiful blonde hair around the side of her neck.

"Well, he could be single," said Dianne and almost clasped her hand over her mouth. She could hardly believe she just said that. There was a slight pause, then Cindy and Gretchen both roared with laughter.

"I like her!" said Cindy. "She's quick."

The conversation over dinner was pleasant and fun. The women enjoyed each other's company, although Gretchen and Cindy might have been enjoying themselves a little too much. They continued to drink heavily and talk louder and louder.

"Oh, Dianne, I wanted to thank you for that lady you sent me: Gen. It's difficult to find a good social worker. The kids just love her. Usually, children are strangely scared of social workers, but they just love her."

"Who's this? And why did you give her to them?" Cindy teasingly asked Dianne. "Our social worker is terrible. She just needs to retire."

"Gen, Gen. What is her name? It's an unusual name," Gretchen said to herself.

Dianne just sat there, quietly pretending not to remember Genesis' name. Then it came to Gretchen. "Genesis. Genesis McGuffey. What a sweet girl."

Just then Cindy began to cough on her beer. "Genesis. I know that name. Does she have a scar on her face?"

"I don't remember her having any scars," offered Dianne quickly.

"Yeah, I don't remember any scars either," said Gretchen.

"What was her last name again?" asked Cindy.

"McGuffey," said Gretchen. "Why? Who are you thinking of?"

"We had this patient. You know, Chris only sees special patients," she looked at Gretchen then at Dianne. "She left against medical advice, but not like legally. She just left. Disappeared. Oh, yeah, she had dreads. A blonde girl with dreads. Does your girl have dreads?"

"Oh no. She's got long, straight hair. She does have blonde hair, though."

"I'm still going to check to see that patient's last name. How many Genesis' could possibly live in Minneapolis," said Cindy, suspiciously.

Dianne's foot began to tap nervously under the table. Dianne picked up her phone and checked the time. "I'm sorry, guys. I've got to go, but I've had a great time. And it was so nice meeting you, Cindy," said Dianne and smiled. Then she slipped out of the restaurant quickly.

Dianne had not been to the parking garage for years. The Partakers were only to go there if there was an emergency. This was an emergency. But when she arrived at the garage no one was there.

Barbara walked out back and slipped a sat phone out from under her flannel. "You said to call you if anything strange ever happened. Well, I've got two men, a woman, and a baby in my home right now. I think they are fugitives. Probably Ints. Not many violent criminals travel with babies." Barbara paused and listened for a moment. "Thanks for calling it in," said Barbara. "I'll be waiting for you." Barbara turned off the phone and slipped it back under her flannel and returned to the house.

Grant and Boxer returned late from the airport that night. It was going to be an all-nighter. He had a report to write for Major Arson about the work camp in Louisiana, and he needed to start gathering intel on Michelle Brice, but all he could think about was Genesis. He looked at his watch. Midnight. He opened up his computer and began plunking at the keys. Plunk, plunk, plunk. He shut the computer. He felt like a teenager. What was happening to him? He was losing all his coolness. He grabbed his keys and headed for the car.

Ten minutes later, Grant pulled up in front of the food and beer mart below Genesis' apartment. He couldn't knock on her door at this time of night. He was certain it would frighten her. He looked around. There were only two customers in the food mart that he could see. He looked down the street, up the street, and behind him. Not many cars around. He considered leaving. "Oh well," he thought to himself. "I drove all the way over here. I might as well." Grant got out of the car but reached back in and started honking the horn. "Honk, honk," echoed loudly off the walls of the street. "Honk, honk, honk," he kept watching her window. He saw someone glance out of the food mart. Grant smiled back at him. "Honk, honk, honk," an older woman slowly pulled a curtain aside in the apartment next to Genesis. "Honk, honk, honk." It just occurred to him, he didn't know if she was a light sleeper or a heavy sleeper. He could be at this all night. "Honk, honk, honk." Finally, he saw Genesis' blinds go up. He began waving frantically and then honked a couple more times. Genesis looked down and saw Grant and instantly disappeared. By the time he shut his car door and looked up, he saw Genesis running around the corner in a full sprint. Before he was quite ready for it, she had jumped into his arms, and he knew then, she was worth looking like a fool for. He wrapped his arms around her and whispered her name over and over. They sat on the curb and talked and laughed until 3 a.m. when she finally kissed him good night. She waved from the window, so he knew she was in safe, and then Grant slowly drove back to the garage, savoring every moment they had spent together.

CHAPTER 21

Do not forget to show hospitality to strangers, for
by so doing some people have shown hospitality to
angels without knowing it.
Hebrews 13:2

Grant returned to the garage and slept for three hours then woke to work on his report. By 9 a.m., dressed in his fatigues, Grant went to ACI to drop off his report to Major Arson. When he entered her office, another officer was leaving.

Grant held the file and stood at attention. "What have you got?" she asked.

Grant handed her the file with his report in it.

"Summarize it."

"There is a man named Stephen at the facility. He fancies himself a prophet. I'd call him a nut. He talks to people about Jesus, and they walk away. Most people just want out of there and don't want any more trouble. Warden Ledbetter runs an excellent facility. It is organized, controlled, and he works them too hard for any congregating. There are two other Ints that follow Stephen around like puppy dogs. The three of them are ostracized by the rest. The guards seem to have this guy under control. I wouldn't let them out for good behavior, but I also don't see them as effective religious leaders. They are well placed in work camp #07."

"Good. I don't have time to manage Ints that are already incarcerated. I have ones out there undermining everything we are trying to accomplish in this country. That's what I need to be focused on. There's some Ints that are being brought in from Canada. Report here at 8 p.m. tomorrow. They should be here by then. Have you got anything on the other assignment I gave you?"

Grant tried not to react when he heard of Ints being brought in from Canada but felt a tremor go through his entire body. "Do you know anything about the Ints from Canada?"

"Two men, a woman, and a baby. Do you have anything yet on the other assignment?" Major Arson looked up in an annoyed manner.

"Not yet. I have two leads I'm following up today. I'll know more by tomorrow evening," Grant replied.

"Good. You're dismissed."

Grant exited Major Arson's office and stopped by Neil's desk. "Neil, how's it going?" asked Grant. "What did I miss while I was gone?"

"Major Arson has been intense. But like more intense. She has started a new small department that Major Brice approved. You know about her and Major Brice, right? That they're a thing," he said as he raised his eyebrows then made kind of a sickened face.

"No. I didn't," replied Grant, guarding his expression.

"It's called FI, forced interrogations. It's in what used to be the medical room at the back of this building. Anyway, we've had nine people go through there then get shipped out. It has freed Major Arson up but doubled my paperwork load," said Neil. "She's searching for some sort of homeland terrorist cell she thinks is right here in Minneapolis."

"I'm going to need the names of those nine people and where they ended up," said Grant. "Just text that to me. I've got some leads I have to follow up, but I'll be back tomorrow evening at eight. There are some Ints coming in from Canada. Do you have the names of those people yet?" asked Grant.

"No. But I can text you those, too, when I get them," replied Neil.

"Thanks, Neil. Have a good day," said Grant. Grant went to the Lord immediately. "Jesus, help me. Direct my path. Protect Your people. If the Panthers are in trouble, speak to Darrell and Lorenzo. I trust You, Lord, with these people. I trust You, Lord, with my life. I am Your bond servant, Jesus. Use me."

Grant pulled out the wiped phone that Warden Ledbetter had given him and called his dad. He explained his concerns and told him to contact him immediately if anyone came to the garage with any messages.

Grant stopped by his room on the east side of Minneapolis. It was just a studio apartment, simple and organized. He probably lived like he was still in the military. It was just what he was accustomed to. He left his tight white t-shirt on and slipped into some denim jeans and pulled on some construction boots. He threaded a belt through the loops of his jeans then glanced at his watch. "Gotta go," thought Grant to himself. "No time for eating. I need to be praying." He stuffed a few items into his backpack that he would need for the day and headed out the door.

He passed his car and headed for the bus stop in front of the Aldi's. He glanced at his watch again. Ten minutes to pray. Grant bowed his head. He noticed someone sit down next to him but was really too deep in prayer to want to make small talk. He had so much on his mind right now.

"Excuse me," said the man next to him. He was a very dark-skinned man. Maybe in his early twenties. "Hey, I forgot my wallet, and I need to get on this bus. Can you loan me a few dollars, please," he said in a thick Nigerian accent.

"Sure," said Grant as he pulled out his wallet and retrieved a twenty-dollar bill. "Now, you've got dinner too," said Grant. "Sometimes, I leave in a rush and forget what's most important, too," said Grant with a smile.

"Hey," the young man said to get Grant's attention. Then he looked directly into Grant's eyes and said, "Don't forget what's most important to Him. It is impossible to please God without faith. In the next twenty-four hours, your team will need you. Trust in the Lord and the training He has given you. You will know exactly what to do when the time comes. Don't second guess it," said the man. "And thank you for dinner." He laid a strong hand on Grant's back and smiled encouragingly, then walked away. Grant wanted to go after the man and ask him a million questions, but the bus pulled up. It's air brakes squealed to a stop, and the door whooshed open. He looked at the man walking away and then at the door one more time. He knew he had to get on the bus. Grant reluctantly stood up and climbed the steps.

Once on, he sat down in an aisle seat by himself, across from a middle-aged Asian woman. She sat uprightly in her seat reading a book. Her black hair covering much of her face as she read. She put the book in her lap and rested her weary head back in her seat. Grant had worked with Jin previously but had never met her in person. She would only agree in the past to meet with Boxer. When she laid her hands on her book, Grant caught a glimpse of the mark on the back of her right hand. And their eyes met briefly.

Grant put his head back in his chair and began to pray, "Jesus, she is marked! Why is she marked? Is it a real one? Can I trust her? Should I just get up and leave? Is this information that critical?"

Jin watched Grant. She knew exactly what he was doing. He was praying. He was praying to this God that seemed so real to some people. But for her, God was the wind; difficult to see, difficult to follow, sometimes here and other times there. But this man was beseeching his God just as she had seen her mother do so many times. She studied him a moment longer, hoping to figure out how to have what he and her mother had, and a tear slid down her face. Grant turned and looked at her. She tilted her head and mouthed, "It's okay. You can trust me." Grant saw the tear and smiled.

The bus jerked to a stop, and the door whooshed open. Jin stood up and walked away, leaving the book behind. At the next stop, Grant grabbed the book and exited the bus.

Grant walked three miles to a small neighborhood across from an elementary school. He stopped and pulled a large square iPad from his backpack and a yellow reflective vest. After slipping on the vest, he began to walk to each house and pretend to enter in their water usage onto the iPad. He checked his watch. It was 2:30 p.m. There was still plenty of time for him to walk through Michelle Brice's home before she left work. He walked over to the meter and checked his surroundings. He walked under the deck at the back of the house and entered the through the sliding glass door in the walk out basement. He made his way upstairs to the kitchen area and then found the den by the front door. Michelle Brice's computer was on the desk. He glanced out the window for any movement. He pulled a thumb drive out of his backpack. He plugged it into the port and began downloading all the files. Grant glanced around the room for any cameras. Just then, a bright yellow school bus stopped at the street corner, and he heard the chatter of kids as they exited the bus. Two girls walked down the street, but three guys stood across the street talking. Grant waited for the drive to complete the download then grabbed it and went back out the way he came.

CHAPTER 22

I consider that our present sufferings are not worth comparing with the glory that will be revealed in us.

Romans 8:18

Grant spent the evening pouring over papers Jin had left for him in the book. There were numbers from bank accounts of dozens of people related to Michelle Brice. Michelle's accounts were clean as a whistle. She had a loser brother not worth two nickels. She had aunts and uncles all over Minnesota. There was a grandpa in Canada, and her mother was in New Zealand. "That's weird, New Zealand. No one else lived outside of the United Americas," thought Grant to himself. He studied the deposits and withdraws. "Grandma is rich! Jackpot!" Grant ran his hands through his hair and bent over the papers. "Now, does grandma have new money or old money?" Grant asked himself. "Grandma makes quite the income. A steady $20,000 a month. How old is grandma? Born in 1933. Grandma is ninety-seven years old and making more money than I do or could ever dream to." Grant scratched at his five o'clock shadow that was getting a little shaggy and itchy. "Where's all the money coming from, Grandma?" he said out loud. "Pension from a rich husband, maybe? Wait a minute, Iceland? Why would someone in Iceland send Grandma money? Let's look at next month. $20,000 from New Zealand? $20,000 from the European Union? $20,000 from England? $20,000 from Australia?"

Grant pulled out his wiped cell phone and called a friend of his from California who was a vice president at Chase before the government took over all the banking in the United Americas. "Mike, hey, it's Grant. How ya doing, buddy? Yes, my dad is great. How are the kids?" After a few more minutes of catching up, he asked Mike to write down the following routing numbers. Mike was more than happy to be a resource and use the knowledge that, at one time, had made him rich on this earth. But Mike had traded all his earthly riches for eternal riches in heaven. Mike lost everything he had on this earth when he wouldn't comply as a government employee and take the mandatory chip. "Mike, does anything about these numbers stick out to you?" asked Grant.

"Can you tell me anything about them?" inquired Mike.

"They all made a very large deposit in an elderly woman's bank account overseas. Not at the same time. Each one on a different month," said Grant.

"Hmmmm. That's strange. How old is she?" asked Mike.

"She's ninety-seven years old."

"This is just a front for someone else to hide money," said Mike.

"How can you tell?" asked Grant.

"Well, if it was larger than $20,000 it would have sent up a red flag to the international community, and they would've started investigating. I'm kinda surprised no one has caught it already. But since these are all government deposits, maybe they know what it is, and they aren't concerned," said Mike.

"What? Government agencies are depositing the money? How can you tell?" asked Grant incredulously.

"I can tell from the first three digits in the routing number. We did lots of work with Great Britain and Australia. Yeah, I recognize most of these government accounts," said Mike.

"Thank you so much for this information, Mike. Say hello to your wife for me." Grant pushed the end call button and stood up and paced around the room.

"Now, the why. Why is she getting all this money?" he said to himself. He walked over to his backpack and retrieved the thumb drive and began to load it onto his computer.

He went through file after file. Grant thought to himself, "Lots of school stuff. She has a teenage boy. That must have been one of the boys I saw get off the bus. Work projects, family stuff. Email." He scrolled down through Michelle Brice's email. No Grandma. She never emails Grandma. I wish I had her phone. Ah, her text messages are on here. She does have a thing going on with Major Arson. But no texting to Grandma. Well, Grandma is ninety-seven. I suppose she doesn't text. Google. Let's see what you google in your spare time. Politics. Politics. Politics. Democratic societies. How to build a Republic. How to overturn a government. Leadership. Freedom of speech. The People's Republic. Michelle Brice is not a communist! She is high up, in a communist military and yet not a communist at heart. She has ambitions. She wants to lead. She wants to lead America back to a free country. All the governments depositing money in her grandma's account are the only democratic societies left. She's a spy! She is working with other countries to free America!"

Grant's mind was spinning, trying to wrap his head around everything he had discovered. "Could God use a woman like this to restore America? Could God use a woman who was a lesbian? Should he report all of this? Should he report just some of this? Major Arson will have her arrested and killed if she learns of this. Should I warn Michelle?"

In an instant, Grant was on his knees. "Jesus, Jesus, this is bigger than I am. I don't know what to do with this information. How did I get myself here? Any way I turn, I feel like I'm compromising. I am unclean. The people around me are unclean. Cleanse me, Lord. Help me to see the way clearly."

Grant was now prostrate before the Lord. His prayers pouring out like a babbling brook before his Heavenly Father. Then everything was still, and Grant knew what to do.

Grant returned to his computer. He began writing the report, the full report. Then he called Michelle Brice.

It was 6 a.m., when Grant fell asleep on his bed with his white t-shirt, jeans, and construction boots still on. Grant woke up with a start at 2 p.m.

His phone was blowing up. Calls from Boxer. Calls from Michelle Brice. Calls from Dianne. Calls from Neil.

Text messages: Neil

> *Here are the names you asked for of the nine people while you were in Louisiana and their current locations.*
> *William Lotus deceased city morgue*
> *Francis Lotus deceased city morgue*
> *Jeremiah Ross deceased city morgue*
> *Rachael Lewis deceased city morgue*

Dante Marshal deceased hospital morgue
Yolanda Marshal deceased city morgue
Isaac Fisher deceased hospital morgue
Trent Hutchinson deceased hospital morgue
Lauren Hayes deceased city morgue

No names of the Ints coming in from Canada yet.

"Please, Jesus, no more dying. Have mercy on us." Grant didn't have time to listen to the calls. He dressed in his fatigues quickly. He printed out his report and grabbed the thumb drive, his keys, and his wallet and headed out the door. He raced to the garage. When he pulled in, he listened to the final message. He thought to himself, "Who is Dianne?"

Then he heard, "This is Dianne. I am the human resources director at the East Bank Hospital." Grant remembered her immediately. "I think nurse Cindy, Dr. Houston's nurse, might figure out who Genesis is. I tried to hide it, but if Cindy digs deeper Genesis' cover might get blown."

Grant slammed both hands on the steering wheel in anger. "Please, Jesus, keep her safe." He pulled his keys and hustled inside without checking around first.

CHAPTER 23

*Be strong and courageous. Do not be afraid or ter-
rified because of them, for the Lord your God goes
with you; he will never leave you nor forsake you.*

Deuteronomy 31:6

"Dad! Dad!" Grant shouted as he entered the storage
unit.

"I'm here, son." said Boxer as he appeared around
the corner.

"We need to pray," said Grant.

"Take courage, my son. What is wrong?" asked Boxer.

Grant pulled out his phone and began to read out
loud the nine names.

William Lotus deceased city morgue
Francis Lotus deceased city morgue
Jeremiah Ross deceased city morgue
Rachael Lewis deceased city morgue
Dante Marshal deceased hospital morgue

Yolanda Marshal deceased city morgue
Isaac Fisher deceased hospital morgue
Trent Hutchinson deceased hospital morgue
Lauren Hayes deceased city morgue

"Grant, check your thinking!" Boxer said rebuking him. "You are just a man. You are not God. Repent. You did not create them. You did not breathe life into them. You do not sustain them, and you could not choose the day they would die. And are they not in a better place? Are they not part of the great cloud of witnesses now, watching you run your race? Go, my son, and do what the Lord has commanded you to do. Take courage in our Lord! Fix your eyes on Him. We are at war! There will be many casualties. But you did not take their lives. These are the schemes of the enemy, so be on guard. Protect your mind so you can see clearly. Be strong and courageous. Now go and be comforted, for I will be praying for you without ceasing," said his father. They embraced, and Grant turned to leave, greatly encouraged in the grace of the Lord.

Grant inhaled deeply then exhaled slowly. He entered ACI but this time it felt like he was entering the den of Hell itself. He greeted Neil with a nod. Neil looked helplessly overwhelmed in paperwork and barely acknowledged Grant's presence. Grant entered Major Arson's office. Major Arson was sitting back in her chair, relaxed. Grant looked closer and saw what he thought was a smile. This unnerved Grant for a moment, and then he recognized it for what it was worth: not much. It was not worth much, this momentary victory she was enjoying. It would end in Jesus' final victory. Major Arson would kneel before Him and call Him the King of kings, and the Lord's revenge would be sufficient. In the moment, he felt sorry for her. She didn't see how Satan had deceived her. How her blind ambition would cost her everything.

"I hope you brought me good news," said Major Arson. "It's been one of my most productive weeks here at ACI. Tell me you have good news."

Grant handed Major Arson the file. "I believe you will find it most satisfying, if I understand you correctly."

"What does the report say?" asked Major Arson, leaning forward on her desk in new interest.

"Lieutenant Major Brice is a spy," said Grant flatly.

Major Arson sat there in silence. Contemplating why Officer Panther would say something so absurd. Then she began wondering if anything so audacious could actually be true. "Explain," was all she could manage to get out.

"She is not a communist. She wants to see the United Americas return to a democratic society. Her ambition is to be the one to lead this new society. She has been working with all the major democratic countries remaining to try to accomplish this," said Grant.

"How do you know this?" demanded Major Arson.

"She has an overseas account in her mother's name, and she is receiving $20,000 a month from various democratic nations," replied Grant flatly.

"This is outrageous!" Grant watched her face as Major Arson went through emotions of anger, betrayal, disbelief, and rage. Then Major Arson stood up and began pacing the room back and forth behind Grant, while he stood at attention. He took no pleasure in what he just reported. It will put Michelle Brice's life in serious danger. Grant watched Major Arson sit back down. Her face was twisted in hatred, and her beauty had disappeared. "You're dismissed," she seethed.

Grant left and went straight to Neil's desk. He looked up at Grant. His eyes looked hollow and wild. "Are you okay?" asked Grant.

"No. This position is not really what I was expecting. I did backgrounds on nine men and women, and now I'm doing transcripts on their interrogations, and soon I will be doing reports on their deaths. And now I have five more backgrounds I have to do, and I assume I will be doing reports on their deaths, too. No, I'm not doing very well. These people looked harmless. They didn't look like criminals," said Neil.

Grant interrupted, "Did you just say you have five more backgrounds to do? Are those the people you said were from Canada? I thought there were four people? Are they here right now?" Grant's voice grew more demanding with every question, and he noticed Neil backing up a bit.

"Yes, they are here; at least some of them. Some of them are at East Bank Hospital. One person is from here in Minneapolis," Neil nervously reported.

"I need names, Neil," Grant said through gritted teeth.

Neil anxiously shuffled through his stacks of paperwork. "Here they are: Trevor Mills, Autumn Mills, Melissa Mills, Darrell Drake, and Genesis McGuffey," said Neil.

Grant's head began to swim as heard Darrell's name, and he nearly vomited when he thought of the danger that Genesis could be in. But all that vanished, and his military training returned. "Where are they, Private Neil?" Grant asked firmly.

"Trevor and Autumn are still here in the F1 area that I told you about. Melissa, Darrell, and Genesis are being transported to East Bank Hospital," Neil quickly reported.

Grant ran to the back of the facility, his AR-15 bouncing on his back with each step. He finally reached what used to be the medical area. He was surprised to find much of the facility still looked like a medical area with IV bags, special boxes for hazardous materials, gloves, and etc. He looked frantically for any of his brothers or sisters. Finally, at the back of the room, he saw two gurneys. First, he saw Autumn strapped to the gurney, not moving. She was beaten and swollen. He checked for a pulse, but he knew he wouldn't find one. He went to grasp her hand in sorrow and found two of her fingers broken and misshapen. He quickly went to the second gurney and saw Trevor, or whom he thought was Trevor. Trevor's face was so swollen he hardly looked human. Grant's mind flashed to the times he checked in on Trevor during his training for the journey to the refugee camp. He was so full of hope and strength. Grant saw a back entrance and left.

His car blasted to the hospital. He didn't even slow at stop lights. He prayed them all green. He took corners at screeching speed. Moments later, he was at East Bank Hospital under the awning marked *Emergency*. He knew the hospital building well. He walked past the receptionist desk just slow enough to catch Everest's eye and nod. Then he sprinted for the stairs. He went to the tiny waiting room where he first met Genesis. He remembered her dreads, her scar, her beautiful eyes.

Then he went to the OR. He blasted through the doors with his broad shoulders and looked around at the faces and then the gurney. Darrell was unconscious on the gurney.

The doctor jumped, startled by the banging doors in his otherwise serene surgical room. "Who are you?" asked the doctor. Nurse Cindy, the anesthesiologist, and another nurse all backed away from Grant.

Grant looked at the anesthesiologist and barked, "Revive him! Revive him, right now."

"I... can't do that we just put him under," stammered the doctor.

Grant's pistol swung from his hip like liquid and pointed squarely at the anesthesiologist. "I said, revive him."

The man began working, immediately. The others just watched in shock as the doctor's hands shook wildly as he added the medicine to Darrell's IV. Within seconds, Darrell's eyes were open.

Grant said loudly. "Give him something to make him alert, right now!"

The man began adding more fluid. Within seconds, Darrell was sitting up looking around.

"Grant?" he said with a heavy slur. His face was badly beaten, and his swollen lips could barely form the word.

"Darrell, we are leaving, right now. I need you to take my AR-15 and follow me," Grant said slowly and clearly.

Grant pointed the gun briefly at nurse Cindy. "Get him his clothes."

Darrell flinched as he got off the gurney. He couldn't stay upright but bent slightly. He spit blood onto the floor. "Okay. I got this Grant. Let's go," said Darrell.

"I need to get Genesis and the baby. We've got to get Genesis. You hold these guys here. They must be across the hall in prep." Grant crossed the hall and, just inside, he saw his love. He unbuckled her wrists carefully. One forearm appeared to be broken. He saw her face cut and bruised. She slowly looked over at him.

She smiled and cringed in pain simultaneously. "I knew you'd come," she whispered. He grabbed her bag of clothes under the gurney. He found the baby in a hospital bassinet not far away from Genesis.

"Are you able to follow me?" asked Grant. Genesis nodded her head yes, but after crossing the hall, she collapsed on the floor. Grant handed the baby to Darrell. He bent down and effortlessly hoisted Genesis over his shoulder. He looked over at Darrell and said, "Let's go."

Grant and Darrell backed out of the room and went for the stairs. As they entered the first floor, people gasped and screamed. Some people pulled their phones out to record this unusual scene. They exited the building with their guns swinging in all directions protectively. In front of the hospital, Everest was waiting in her red convertible. They climbed in. Everest sped away.

Grant pulled out the phone and called Boxer. Boxer answered on the first ring. "Dad, I've got Genesis, the baby, and Darrell. Everest is with us also. We need to leave Minneapolis immediately. Send a message to the Panthers to be on alert and not to contact any of us. Tell them they are on their own but never alone. Tell them I love them. Dad, come with one of the vans to Mike's Deli. We will meet you in back. Hurry. I love you, Dad."

"I'm so proud of you, son. Well, done. I will see you soon," said Boxer.

That was the last time Grant spoke to his beloved father.

CHAPTER 24

Do not be like them, for your Father knows what
you need before you ask him.
Matthew 6:8

This hurting group of believers ditched the red convertible and walked half a block down an alley to Mike's Subs. Grant carried Genesis. When they finally arrived, they all slumped to the ground, except Everest.

Everest held Lissa and walked and bounced her the best she could, but she didn't have any children of her own, and she just never really understood kids. Everest lived at the feet of her heavenly Father. Grant often teased her for only having one foot here on earth. Everest was completely taken with the Lord and didn't seem to have a desire for a husband or children.

Lissa continued to fuss. She was hungry, and nothing was going to satisfy her but some milk. Darrell sat on the asphalt and held his aching head with one hand and his broken ribs with the other hand. Genesis was slouched up against a wall going in and out of consciousness.

Grant and Mike flung open the back screen door to the restaurant. Grant had a bottle of milk in hand. Everest gratefully took the bottle, and Lissa finally quieted.

Mike looked around at the group. "She needs prayer," he said as he looked at Genesis.

"I agree," said Grant. "Could you pray, Mike?" Before Mike made subs, he was a head pastor at Gateway Church. Boxer was also a pastor there. It was the only church Grant had ever attended.

Mike and Grant laid hands on Genesis. Darrell and Everest joined them. Moments later, Genesis began to sit up and look around. Her left eye drooped. Her swollen lips had two cuts on them. She winced as she unknowingly moved her arm. Mike wrapped his hands gently around Genesis' wrist, and the group began to pray once more. The Lord showed up in a mighty way. Her arm shifted back together. The group praised God in awe and wonder, forgetting briefly the peril they still faced.

Grant stepped away from the group. He took out his phone and called Boxer. It rang once, twice, and at the third ring the call connected, and the voice Grant heard sent tremors of rage through his body.

"Grant, is that you? I was just asking your father where you were. Geez, you don't look anything like him.

It took a minute for him to share that information with us," said Major Arson.

"How did you find him?" seethed Grant.

"You might not be chipped, but I did have your work phone monitored. It wasn't hard to find your most recent locations then. I asked your dad how he wanted to go, and he simply kneeled and began muttering, 'Jesus.' I put a bullet in the back of his head," Major Arson said coldly.

"Nooooooooo!" screamed Grant as he fell to knees, weeping.

"Have you gotten anything to eat at Mike's yet? You know, I'm going to kill Mike and his family too, right?" Major Arson said matter-of-factly.

Grant dropped the phone. He slammed both hands on the ground and bowed his head. "This is what you have called me to, and my life is yours. Make me strong and courageous. Not by power, nor by might, but by Your Spirit," proclaimed Grant. He looked at Mike who had rushed to Grant's side. Grant stood up tall and breathed in air, deep in his lungs then said, "They are almost here. They are going to kill you and your family. Grab your family and leave everything. Is this your van?" Grant asked, looking at a large delivery van.

"Yes," said Mike quickly.

"Go, man! Go!" hollered Grant.

Everest, Lissa, and Genesis got into the van. Darrell and Grant covered both alley entrances with their weapons. Mike and his wife burst through the back screen door of the restaurant and got in the van. Mike tossed Grant the keys. Darrell was the last one in. Grant ordered everyone to get down and stay down. He grabbed the Mike's Subs hat beside him and put it on. Then he pulled onto the main street.

Major Arson already had a five-mile perimeter set around Mike's Subs. Grant slowed the van as he approached a newly set up roadblock. They were releasing dogs. The dogs were circling the vehicle in front of them as a peace officer asked the driver some questions. Grant said, "Pray, people. Pray." They already were. The steady hum of their whispers gave Grant the courage he needed. He rolled down his window. He looked at the German Shepherd sniff the air and pause. Right as the dog opened his mouth to bark, a huge blast came from two buildings down, and the earth shook. The praying believers didn't know it, but the Lord answered their prayers before they even asked. The building two hundred yards away was scheduled for demolition today. The demolition was postponed three times that day, but it blasted exactly when the Lord sovereignly purposed it to. As the earth shook, the peacekeepers grabbed their ears and ran for cover, not knowing what exactly just happened. Grant coasted through the perimeter. He looked in the rearview mirror and saw the city block covered with dirt and dust. Grant said to himself, "Did you see that, Dad? Did you just see what God did?" He smiled and pushed that van to its max speed straight west.

Stephen and Kendall sat down at the corner booth at Denny's. "Mark should be here soon. He's got a further drive than we do," said Stephen.

"Do you know what this is all about?" asked Kendall.

"He said he didn't want to say over the phone. He sounded somewhere between terrified and excited. There he is now," said Stephen.

The tall, gangly man who looked like a marathoner weaved his way through the tables to them.

"Brothers, it is good to see you both. We must hurry and open this conversation in prayer," said Mark with a smile but bypassing hugs and handshakes. They bowed their heads. "Lord we need you here with us. Guide our footsteps. We need you before us and behind us. Amen."

"Let me speak, quickly. We have been compromised; the entire work camp. Officer Grant has been discovered. He had to do a rescue operation to get three of his people out. You can watch it on the news this evening.

He has lost twelve of his Partakers including Boxer, who was his father. Grant's father was murdered execution style by Major Arson. Major Arson found one of our clean phones on Boxer and contacted Grant with the phone. If she's smart, it is only a matter of time before she figures out we provided him with the phone. That leaves us with an issue of time, supplies, men, and location and transportation."

Mark had Stephen and Kendall's full attention. They all leaned forward on the table. "Let's deal with time first. As I see it, we at best, have between two to twelve hours to move our men. After that, Major Arson could have troops at our doorstep. We have military on sight, but not enough present, to secure four hundred plus men. I don't believe she will use them until they have backup. How quickly do you think we can be ready to vacate the premises?" asked Mark.

"I can't believe this is happening," said Kendall as he ran his hands across the back of his neck. "I would say four hours," responded Kendall.

"Next, we need to talk about supplies. We need as many clean phones as we can get. We have one semi already docked with kits for the morning and another one packed and ready to go with completed phones. We will need to take food, medicine, clothing, towels, and kitchen supplies. Kendall, is there any way to get into the armory?"

"Certainly. I'll oversee that myself," said Kendall.

"I'll get a crew to pack the other supplies," said Stephen.

"Transportation should be easy. We will pack the men into the semis. It will be uncomfortable, but praise God, we have transportation. Since I will be the only one who knows our destination, I will drive in front of the semis, and I'll have you two follow the semis."

"That brings us to our next topic: location. This cannot be released to any of the men for our safety and the safety of our host. There is a rancher in Texas. He has a thousand acres. He is willing to hide us. Praise God. His name is Matthew Raven. Maybe you've heard of him," said Mark with a smirk.

The two men sat in utter shock looking at Mark.

"The actor?" they asked, simultaneously.

"Yes, indeed," replied Mark.

"Next is men. We need a head count of men. We need this explained to them clearly. They need to understand there will not be contact with the outside world. They may not see their wives and children for years. They may never see them again," said Mark solemnly. "And that goes for you two, also."

Stephen said, "I will brief my disciplers. They know their men well. Kendall can call them to their work cells. There, the disciplers can pray with them and explain the situation. They can get people signed up, and we should have numbers shortly thereafter."

"What about those that stay behind?" asked Kendall.

"They will have the choice to stay in their cell and be interrogated by ACI or take their chances on their own, hiding from the government. There are no easy options. We are living in the last days. Persecution and suffering await us all. It is important that the men are not pressured or demeaned, no matter their choice. We love them regardless, and we will continue to pray for each other to be strong in the faith until the end," said Mark, looking between the two other men, who nodded in agreement.

"I need to know if you are in, all the way. There's no turning back after this. This is not an easy decision for any of us. My wife passed two years ago, but I have two grown children I may never see again. Stephen you are single, but I'm sure you have family and friends you will be leaving behind. And what about you Kendall?" asked Mark.

"My wife divorced me five years ago when the work camp was sucking the life out of me. My children are grown, but they are pretty angry with me about the divorce. I don't have a lot left here in Louisiana," said Kendall. "I'm in," said Kendall, confidently.

"I'm in, too," said Stephen with a smile.

"Praise God! I was hoping you would both say that. Grant has a master plan for cells that are popping up all over the country to unite us. Once we are settled in Texas, he will contact us. This will be the journey of a lifetime. Though we walk through the valley of the shadow of death, we will fear no evil."

CHAPTER 25

"For I know the plans I have for you," declares the
Lord, "plans to prosper you and not to harm you,
plans to give you hope and a future."
Jeremiah 29:11

Genesis slipped into the front seat of the van. She
flipped down the visor and saw herself for the first time
in the glowing mirror. Tears started silently and un-
controllably flowing from her eyes. One eye was droop-
ing, and a pool of bright red blood was in the white of
her eye. She remembered being pushed to the ground
while her hands were cuffed behind her. Her lips were
swollen. She remembered the taste of blood after he
had punched her and the way her head and neck had
whipped to the side. She ran her hand soothingly up
and down the muscles of her neck. Grant took his eyes
off the road for a moment and glanced over at her, and
she saw his tears.

"I'm so sorry. I'm so, so sorry. They hurt you. I never wanted you to get hurt. But I still have you with me, and I am so very grateful," said Grant, and he reached over and gently placed his hand on her cheek.

"I feel old," said Genesis softly. "Between the loss of my family and this, I feel like I'm old. Not in a bad way, but a good way. In my suffering, He was there. Jesus was there. I never felt alone. In fact, I felt strong. I became stronger with every strike, with each kick. And I wasn't angry. There was just peace. And the pain; it passed, but the reality of His kingdom never passed. My faith feels like someone who has lived a dozen lives. Everything I've professed since the loss of my family I know now is true. My faith has been tested," she said with a small smile as she looked at Grant.

"The joy in the midst of suffering," said Grant knowingly. "Yes. I know Jesus like that, too."

"Boxer is gone, isn't he?" asked Genesis.

"Yes. He is gone from this earth and in the presence of Jesus. He is at peace and where he always longed to be. I miss him. My heart feels broken and heavy."

Genesis hid her face in her hands and wept. Yet another loss. "I loved him, too," said Genesis. There was a long silence as they both remembered what Boxer meant to each of them.

"We both knew you when you were just a child," said Grant. Genesis looked up at Grant, confused. Grant continued. "Boxer used to take me to the Children's Hospital at UMMC when I was a teenager to visit sick children there. You were in the hospital for a long time in the burn unit. You were still there when I shipped out with the military. Boxer continued to visit you and keep me updated until, one day, you were gone."

"I'm sorry. I don't remember either of you. I must have been so frightened and traumatized," said Genesis. "That must be why Boxer and I seemed so close even when we first met."

"Yes," said Grant.

"Did you both know who I was right away?" asked Genesis.

"Yes," said Grant. They drove on silently together.

"Do you know where we are going?" Genesis asked as she looked one more time in the mirror and tried to smooth out her hair and clean up the blood from various places on her face.

"God has shown me grand glimpses of many things. I won't tell you or anyone because, if any of us are apprehended, it is better for everyone if they don't know names or locations. But what He has shown me is beyond my capability and beyond my imagination. But I trust Him to bring about what He has shown me," said Grant.

"I love you, Genesis. You are everything you were in my dream and more. I have a lot of things I need to say to you, but first I need to talk to Darrell about some very important and timely things. Could you ask him to come up here, please?" asked Grant.

"Sure," said Genesis. She whispered, "I love you," in his ear and went to the back of the van.

Darrell sat down with a grunt, "Where are we?"

"We are going due north now, on US Route 29. We are almost to Pembina on the edge of Minnesota, North Dakota, and Canada. How are you feeling?" asked Grant as he watched the road.

"Like a truck hit me, then backed up over me. But I'm fine," said Darrell, as he looked out the side window, and a sad memory of the recent traumas crossed his mind.

"You are walking around like you've got a couple of broken ribs," said Grant, concerned.

Darrell laughed, "Well you should see the other guy. I probably do have a couple broken ribs."

"Did you get any sleep the last few hours?" asked Grant.

"Yeah. What have you got planned? I don't think I could run a marathon or anything," replied Darrell suspiciously.

"That's exactly what I have planned," Grant said, with a worried glance over at Darrell. "I have to ask you some hard questions, first." There was a small pause to see if Darrell opposed questioning so soon after his trials, but he said nothing, so Grant continued. "Do you remember what happened to you, Trevor, and Autumn?"

"Yes," said Darrell weakly. "They used Trevor as a tool to get information out of Autumn. They beat him mercilessly. He eventually went unconscious and never came back."

"I hate to ask this, and I don't think anything less of her for it, but did Autumn ever tell them anything?" asked Grant as gently as he could.

"Trevor and Autumn had no idea where we were going. No one did except me. We were only two and a half days into the journey. So we weren't anywhere near the destination," stated Darrell.

"Can you tell me how you got arrested?" asked Grant.

"Oh man, you don't know about Peter," remembered Darrell.

"Ashley and Matt's kid?" asked Grant.

"Yeah," said Darrell, sadly. "Peter and Paul were out exploring at the end of the first day. It was starting to get dark. Peter fell off a fifty-foot cliff and died. We buried him there. That was what Peter's family decided to do. I gave them the option for us all to go back, but they said that continuing on is what Peter would've wanted. The second day was hard because the group was still in mourning, especially Peter's family. Then, little Lissa got sick. She was burning up with a fever, coughing, and crying. Trevor and Autumn tried everything. Finally, we stopped, and I went to see if I could find help. I found a small home in the middle of nowhere. A retired nurse happened to live there. We brought little Lissa to her, and she nursed her back to health, but she's the one who called the authorities," said Darrell.

"Satan appears as an angel of light," Grant said, remembering the prophecy.

"Yep," said Darrell in agreement. "That same thing occurred to me, but by then it was too late. I just don't know if I did the right thing. And now, Trevor, and Autumn are dead, and little Lissa is all alone."

"Darrell, in that same group of prophecies, God called you to lead. He knew your decision and still chose you. We must trust Him and look ahead, not behind." Grant paused to let Darrell consider this, then he said carefully. "Did you give them any information about the Fort Hope Indian Reservation?"

"No. I did give them information, but it was all wrong information," said Darrell.

"Did you see Genesis at all, while you were there?" asked Grant.

"They brought her in after us. Trevor and Autumn were both already dead," said Darrell.

"Did either of you let on that you knew each other?" questioned Grant.

"No. Genesis is smart. She immediately started a distraction when she first saw me, so any sudden, natural reaction was covered. She is the bravest person, Grant, I have ever met. She never flinched, spoke, cried out, or reacted. Her face was glowing. She had the appearance of peace, kindness, and forgiveness even as they beat her. And they mocked her relentlessly. It was as though she grew stronger the more they beat her, but that incensed them even more. But there was nothing she could do to hide it. It's just who she is, or rather who Christ is in her, in the midst of suffering. I was ashamed of myself after seeing her in her suffering," said Darrell.

Grant looked back at Genesis. She was holding little Lissa who was beginning to fuss now. He was filled with admiration, concern, sorrow, and love. She completely overwhelmed him.

"What do you think has happened with Lorenzo and the rest of the group?" asked Grant.

"Before I left with Lissa, Trevor, and Autumn for Barbara's house, the nurse, I gave instructions for Lorenzo if anything went wrong. I told him who the contact was at the reservation and at the refugee camp. I gave him detailed directions to camping and supply locations. Lorenzo is smart and the group is strong. I am confident they will make it there," reported Darrell.

"Okay, that is good news," said Grant. "Darrell, God has given me a vision of what we need to do, and you are a part of that. It seems overwhelming and outrageous, but we need to trust Him and follow the path

He has given us. I am going to drop you off just south of the Canada border and have you cross over on foot. Here is cash to get the supplies you need at a Walmart. I need you to hike to the refugee camp and stay there, permanently. You and Cheyenne are to be the leaders of the Panthers there. You will need to fortify your area. God will show you how to do this. Pray, fast, and trust in Him. God is going to greatly increase your territory there. People will hear about your refugee camp, and they will come from all over Canada. Preach, disciple, and baptize in the name of Jesus. He will provide for all of your needs. Now, I need you to wake up Mike and the others and have them pray for you. You need healing, grace, and strength to make the journey you are about to take. Here is a wiped phone. I will be in touch with you soon. There is more that I will need to tell you," said Grant.

Darrell bowed his head. He appeared to be praying. Then he grasped a hand with Grant, and they smiled knowingly about the danger they have shared and the dangers that were still ahead of them both.

CHAPTER 26

My sheep listen to my voice; I know them, and
they follow me.
John 10:27

Michelle Brice was at the same desk where Grant
was earlier that day, downloading her files. Her phone
rang twice: unknown caller. She almost let the call go
but felt a nudge inside to answer it.

"Hello?" said Michelle. There was a slight pause on
the line, and she almost disconnected the call.

Then Grant said, "Michelle, you need to listen to me
very carefully. Your life and the life of your son will depend on the instructions I'm giving you right now."

"Who is this? I demand to know your name right
now," she commanded. Then Grant heard Michelle yell,
"Trayvon! Trayvon!" Grant could hear the panic in her
voice. "Trayvon!" she yelled again.

"What is it, Mom?" asked Trayvon as he came around
the corner from the kitchen. Michelle motioned for her

son to sit on the floor, and she pulled the Glock from her purse on her desk. Her son's eyes widened.

"My name is Grant Panther."

"How do you know about my son?" demanded Michelle Brice.

"That isn't important right now. Just please listen carefully. Tomorrow, Major Arson is going to find out that you are a spy," said Grant, flatly.

"What are you talking about? That is the most absurd thing I've ever heard of," said Michelle forcefully.

"I know about your mother in New Zealand. I know the different democratic governments that have deposited $20,000 into her account. I know that you are not a communist at heart, and you love your country," said Grant. Michelle was quiet, and Grant had her complete attention.

"How do you know all this?" she asked.

"That is not important right now. If you want you and your son to live, follow my instructions exactly," Grant paused for a moment to see if Michelle objected again, but she waited quietly so Grant continued. "Go to the Minneapolis airport right now. Don't take anything with you other than your passport, your son's passport, and a Bible. Get the next flight to Houston, Texas. Once there, get a cab and go directly to the British consulate and seek political asylum there. They will be able to protect you and your son," he paused again to let her digest everything he just said.

"I know, Michelle, you are not a follower of Jesus Christ, but I'm warning you that the time is short on this earth, so choose carefully who you and your son are going to serve. Repent of your sins and be fully devoted to Jesus, and He will direct your path. He has a major role for you to play in the future of our country, but you must first repent. Major Arson will receive this information tomorrow. You don't have time to waste. Go quickly." Grant ended the call, then closed his eyes and asked the Lord to reveal Himself to Michelle and give her ears to hear.

Michelle Brice and her son, Trayvon, exited the cab in Houston, Texas very late that night and entered the British consulate with nothing but her passport and a book under her arm.

Major Arson returned to her office and went into the restroom. She washed the blood off of her hands and changed out of her work clothes that were stained with the blood from Boxer and put on her fatigues that she always kept in the office. She began pacing the office, then yelled repeatedly for Private Neil. But when Private Neil saw Major Arson storm into the building with a murderous look on her face and blood splattered on her clothes, he removed his side arm and laid it on his desk. He opened his drawer and grabbed his wallet and keys and walked out the front door of the ACI. On the way to his car, he pulled out the card that Officer Panther had given him.

Major Arson went to ACI's war room and began to bark orders. She pointed to two men at the entrance. "I need you and you to find Lieutenant Major Michelle Brice and detain her."

Then she wheeled around to another officer at a computer. "I need you to find the exact location of Officer Panther."

She found another officer standing near the copy machine. "I need you to get to East Bank Hospital and ensure the procedures for Genesis McGuffey, Melissa Mills, and Darrell Drake are completed. Don't move from the surgery doors until it's completed!"

"Officer Panther is at Mike's Subs five miles from here," reported the officer at the computer.

"Get him on speaker. Now!" demanded Major Arson.

She turned to another officer on a computer and said, "I want a five-mile perimeter set up around Mike's Subs. Put an APB out on Officer Grant Panther. I want him apprehended, dead or alive." The officer began typing ferociously on her computer.

The two officers who were at the door returned. "Major Arson, Lieutenant Major Brice is not in her office. She never reported to work today."

She walked over to a third officer on a computer. "Get her on GPS and find out where she is," seethed Major Arson. Major Arson breathed in the adrenaline and breathed out determination. She was in her element. When chaos reigned, she grew even more in control. She could see what needed to be done and achieve it. This was her chance to move up and beyond the ACI, directly to the First Lady. This was the opportunity she had been waiting for.

God's favor was on work camp #07. The entire group of prisoners, the guards, and even the soldiers that guarded the work camp joined their leaders, Stephen, Kendall and Mark, for the journey to Texas. Mark was given a government car and ID. Mark's car, the two semis, and Kendall at the rear all easily passed the check points along the way. They traveled to the far west side of Texas.

They arrived just east of Sanderson, Texas, as the moon was overhead. It was muggy, and the men were stiff and hot from the fourteen-hour trip. The semi doors flew open, and men poured out of the semi like a dam being opened. They were greeted with the screech of cicadas and a warm breeze. They poured out onto an air strip and walked into an empty plane hangar. There were two small engine planes and a helicopter parked outside the large metal building. Inside, the men rejoiced to find four hundred cots and eight-foot fans cooling the building. There were tables and tables of food and water. There were six port-a-potties just out back.

The relief and thankfulness of these men was audible. Dante, a creamy black man with hazel soft eyes, stood six foot and four inches, with a wingspan from heaven, he lifted his arms and his mighty voice to the heavens and shouted, "Hallelujah!" He led the men in a glorious time of praise and worship as their voices thundered through the dry neighboring hills of Texas. Dante's voice was awe-inspiring, and his devotion to worshipping the Lord was second to none. At the back of the hangar, Matt removed his cowboy hat exposing his renoun thick silver hair and leaned upon the metal wall, enjoying the presence of the Lord. He never imagined God would use him or this simple metal building for such a glorious event.

As the men began to quiet before the Lord, Matthew Raven walked humbly to the center of these great men. His hat in his hand, and his dusty boots clunking as he walked. His steely blue eyes mesmerized the men who recognized him from his films. When the men saw who it was, whispers rumbled across the building. Matt welcomed the men. He told them about the property and the men who worked for him, who would be around to help. He hoped they would feel at home here in his dry, dusty hangar. The men thanked him with applause, which appeared to make him uncomfortable. His intention wasn't to receive applause; he felt he had sacrificed very little compared to their endeavors.

As Matthew was heading out, he stopped to talk to Mark and met Stephen and Kendall. Mark said again, "Thank you, Matt, for all you arranged here for the men. It was a difficult journey, and the food and cots are appreciated."

"These are desperate times for our country and her people," said Matthew in his soft Texas drawl. "We need leadership. We need courage right now. I have a friend staying up at the ranch that I think you men are going to want to meet tomorrow. The government of Australia has sent him here to help with communication. As I'm sure you know, Australia invented Wi-Fi, and they have sent you the finest mind from CSIRO to help out. They believe they can set up a bandwidth that is undetectable to our government so that your groups can communicate with each other. They are willing to help any way they can, including money, weapons, and military training."

"How do they know about all of our plans?" asked Mark.

"Apparently, they have a spy in the ACI, and they have recently contacted your leader, Grant Panther," replied Matt. The men looked at each other and smiled. "Well, get some sleep. There will be lots to talk about in the morning. I won't be here for the next month, but there will be men here that will keep you safe. Marcos runs everything here. If you need anything just check with him. It was mighty nice meeting y'all and your men. It's been a blessing to me to be a part of this. Godspeed." The men each shook his hand and said their goodbyes. What could God possibly have planned for tomorrow?

CHAPTER 27

Though one may be overpowered, two can defend themselves, a cord of three strands is not easily broken.
Ecclesiastes 4:12

Grant pulled the van onto a long dirt road. The van bounced over thin, deep grooves in the road. There wasn't a light in the darkness to be seen anywhere except in the glorious stars above. It was late in the evening. Grant had been on the phone with various people almost nonstop. Everest sat beside him taking meticulous notes. Writing down phone numbers and addresses, names and titles of people.

Grant stopped the van in front of a plain two-story white house. There was a large white barn to the back left of the house. Parked beside the barn was a square, black covered wagon with tiny windows and a red reflective triangle on the back. The tired group of people in the van began to shift and rustle about. Grant turned to his friends and said, "Stay here a minute, please. These people have no idea we are coming."

Grant opened the door and heard the neighing of horses. He smelled the strong odor of manure. Crickets chirped as his boots kicked up the dirt as he walked to the front door. Grant knocked on the door. He bowed his head and prayed, "Lord, give us your favor here. We need a time of rest and healing." Grant knocked again. He knew there was nothing to fear in coming to this home in the middle of the night. He would not be met with a gun, or a bat, or even a harsh word. He would be met with grace and love. The door cracked open, and a man Grant's age in a white cotton shirt and dark pants opened the door. The man's beard was down to his collar bone; his thick dark hair was disheveled. "Caleb? Is that you under that mighty beard?" said Grant with a small chuckle.

"Grant? Grant Panther?" the man said with surprise.

Caleb stepped out from behind the screen door and grabbed Grant in a brotherlike hug. "Grant!" Caleb exclaimed. "It is so good to see you, brother. But what in the world are you doing at my doorstep in the middle of the night?"

"It is a very, long story, Caleb. I'm in trouble, and I have a van of people who are hurting and in trouble too," said Grant.

Caleb's eyes went over to the van, and he saw the faces in the van peering back at him.

"You don't have to take us in," said Grant. "We are in trouble with the government. You need to understand that. We are wanted. I don't want to bring any trouble on you and your family."

"There is no government that I fear, my friend, except the heavenly one that I am a citizen of. Come. All of you, come in. I will wake Anna," and Caleb turned and disappeared.

The motley group entered the simple, clean Amish home. Black boots were lined up outside the front door. Inside, black hats of different sizes hung on the wall. They could hear excited whispers in old German coming from up the stairs. Shortly after that, Caleb and Anna came down the stairs and greeted them all. Anna was horrified at the wounds of Genesis. She pulled out a small glass jar with ointment and began treating her wounds at the kitchen table. Anna's hand brushed over Genesis' flowered scar on her face and said softly, "You have had such pain, and yet your beauty just glows. It must be the joy of Jesus in your heart," she whispered gently in her thick, German accent.

Genesis looked into Anna's hazel eyes and said, "Thank you. That is the kindest thing anyone has ever said to me."

Anna just then caught a glimpse of little Lissa. "A baby," she crooned and went over to see her in Everest's arms. "May I hold her, please?" she asked. Everest placed little Lissa in her arms, and Anna began to sway. "Is this your beauty?" she asked Everest.

"No," she replied. "This is little Lissa. Her parents were killed two days ago."

"What? She has no parents?" exclaimed Anna.

"No," Everest replied sadly.

The phone rang and Grant left the room quietly. The wood floorboards creaked, and everyone turned to see a little blonde boy about seven years old enter the kitchen. "Mama," said Levi, "Why are there Englishers here in the middle of the night?"

"They are friends of your Dat's," replied Anna. "Now go get my blueberry pie from the other room and fetch some wood for some coffee." Levi hustled off, happy to not be sent back to bed and hoping for a piece of pie for himself.

Mike approached Caleb and asked if his wife and him could lie down anywhere. Caleb asked them to wait while he made them a pallet on the floor in the back room.

Grant walked back in and whispered some more things to Everest. She pulled out her notebook and began writing.

Anna asked if anyone would mind if she fed little Lissa and put her down for the night. All agreed, and the two disappeared for the remainder of the night. Mike and his wife retired for the evening in the other room, grateful to be able to lay down. Everest soon found a couch and fell asleep. Caleb swooshed Levi off to bed. Then, Grant, Genesis, and Caleb sat down to pie and coffee.

"So how do you two know each other?" asked Genesis looking from Grant to Caleb.

Grant looked at Caleb and laughed, "Well, my brother, Caleb, used to be a bit of a rebel." Genesis lifted an eyebrow in disbelief, and Grant continued with the story. "Caleb, here left the Amish during his teens rumspringa, and after some drinking and tattooing, decided to follow some guys into the military where he found himself completely out of his element."

"Ja," chimed in Caleb. "That's when I met my brother in the Lord, Grant. We served together. He saved my life from the rest of the platoon multiple times. I was a rebellious boy, but not as tough as I thought I was. I couldn't fire a gun, no matter the punishment. They eventually sent me back home, but not before Grant turned me back to our Lord Jesus. We have kept in touch for years through the mail. His letters were like Apostle Paul's letters to me. They were water for my dry soul. I began to study the Word and disciple other Amish men.

Often times, I would butt heads with the elders about traditions and the Word of God. Finally, me and some other families picked up and moved further west here, to go back to farming and further from the temptations of this world." Caleb pulled at his beard gently. "But now, what I really want to know is why Grant Panther is at my door in Montana in the wee hours of the night," crooned Caleb.

Grant began from when he left the military, to his undercover work with the Partakers, to the Panther Refugee Camp, to the Kingdom Workers in Louisiana, to his final rescue mission, Boxer's death, and their escape. In the midst of all the story, Grant had reached under the table and grabbed Genesis' hand. So thankful that she was still alive and at his side.

"You are, indeed, in need of much rest," said Caleb. "That, you will find here. We will talk more of the future tomorrow. I will make you both a pallet on the floor with the others. Never mind the roosters tomorrow. Sleep your fill. My Anna will feed you well," said Caleb. Then he hurried off to find more quilts and pillows.

CHAPTER 28

Do not be afraid of what you are about to suffer.
I tell you, the devil will put some of you in prison
to test you, and you will suffer persecution for ten
days. Be faithful, even to the point of death, and I
will give you life as your victor's crown.
Revelation 2:10

Michelle Brice and her son were given a room to stay in for the night at the British consulate in Houston, Texas. Her son, Trayvon, was in bed for the night, and she was sitting in a chair beside him under a book light. Her Bible was laying in her lap open to Psalm 23. She rubbed her forehead, as if she could push the fear and worries from her mind. All she knew and depended on was a thousand miles away in Minneapolis. She had nothing but these strangers at the consulate and the words of a stranger, "These are the last days...choose carefully" and the only Bible verse she ever remembered: Psalm 23. Her grandmother had read them to her one night as a child, when she had spent the night at her house. They brought her such peace. She read them again, and that same peace returned. "He leads me beside quiet waters, he refreshes my soul... Even though I walk through the darkest valley I will fear no evil, for you are with me."

The next morning, breakfast was brought to their room, and they were asked to attend a meeting with a British Intelligence officer at eleven. He had flown in that morning to speak with Michelle.

Michelle and Trayvon entered a very understated looking office at eleven o'clock. Michelle still had her Bible under her arm. She wasn't sure why she brought it, but at this point, it was the only thing she possessed other than her purse. They sat down across from an older gentleman. He shook both their hands and noticed the Bible beneath her arm. They began to speak of the Lord Jesus. The great price He paid, so that they could be free. Similar to the great price that Michelle and her son would now pay, so that their country could be free. They spoke of a freedom that could never be usurped, never tarnished or stolen. They spoke of a love that was greater than any other love. A love so great, it would forgive any sin, remove all the stains, and make you white as snow. At this, Michelle broke down. She cried for all her sins, the sins of her fellow soldiers, of her past lovers, of her sins that her son bore as well. She wept until she was clean and new and whole. And there, in that office, Michelle and her son prayed with a British Intelligence officer and asked Jesus to be the Lord and Savior of their lives.

Later that evening, Michelle sat down to dinner with that British Intelligence officer and two other officials. The men laid out a plan they had for spreading a democratic message throughout the world, but specifically aimed at the United Communist Americas. This message would prepare the hearts and the minds of the people in the world for the return of North America: the United States of America, Mexico, and Canada. They would provide Michelle with security, staff, speeches, transportation, an income, and an international education for her son. The intelligence officer looked at Michelle and said, "The most important words we want you to declare to the world are the words that we know you hold so dear, that you were willing to risk everything for. We could find no better person to declare to the world:

'We hold these truths to be self-evident, that all men are created equal, that they are endowed by their Creator with certain unalienable Rights, that among these are Life, Liberty and the pursuit of Happiness.—That to secure these rights, Governments are instituted among Men, deriving their powers from the consent of the governed,— That whenever any Form of Government becomes destructive of these ends, it is the Right of the

People to alter or abolish it, and to institute a new Government, laying its foundation on such principles and organizing its powers in such form, as to them shall seem most likely to affect their Safety and Happiness.'"

Michelle looked at the men incredulously. "Why? Why would you care enough to try to reinstate the United States of America? This Declaration of Independence was a Declaration of Independence from Britain?

"Right now, we have an alliance, as you know, of Britain, the European Union, Australia, New Zealand, and Iceland working to overthrow the communist government of the United Communist Americas. These countries are working with several leaders, like yourself in UCA, to supply them with military equipment, training, and technology. Not only would this return North America back to trade and help our countries economically, it would also return to us an important ally and friend. We have the chance to stop the spread of communism and human rights violations. But most importantly, the United States of America can once again be that beacon of light to the world that stands for justice and freedom. It will also spread a message of hope and give other countries a road map out of communism."

"What are the names of these other leaders in UCA?" asked Michelle, who hadn't touched her meal yet.

The men looked at each other in quiet agreement. The intelligence officer said, "Grant Panther will be the leader of the United States of America. Cheyenne Templeton will be the leader of Canada. Lorenzo Garcia will be the leader of Mexico. This is, of course, just until we can set up viable candidates to run for president, and then the people will get to vote and what a glorious and celebrated day that will be. And Stephen Knox will run the military until the three countries can establish their own sovereign militaries again."

"Hmmm. Grant Panther. He is the reason I'm here," said Michelle. "So, what is the next step?" asked Michelle.

"You will travel from major city to major city; country to country. You will be honored as a political refugee from UCA. You will tell of the evils of communism from a first-hand perspective. But most of all, at every rally you will recite the Declaration of Independence. When you are not giving speeches, you will be working with two ghost writers and publish a book. It will be a best seller around the world."

Major Arson entered the enormous round office. The floor-to-ceiling windows lay naked before the purple, majestic mountains in Denver, Colorado. After the swift takeover of the USA, one of the first acts of Lady Crestoff was to move the capital of UCA from Washington D.C. to Denver, Colorado. The mountains screamed strength and provided a natural defense for the new government. The old capital had been gutted, vandalized, and set ablaze during the riots. The government was collapsing, and the new location gave the people a new sense of pride after the embarrassing riots and self-destruction in front of the entire world.

Major Arson ran her hand over the sleek furniture overlooking the gripping view. Her other hand nervously straightened her skirt and touched her bun. Finally, Lady Crestoff entered from a side door with an assistant hustling beside her, trying to anticipate her every need. Lady Crestoff went directly behind her desk but did not sit down. She stood like the mountains regally. Her white hair glowing with a kind of righteousness. Her strong nose and eagle like eyes were impressive and cunning.

"Major Arson. It is good to meet you. You are the hero of UCA this week. Congratulations on a job well done and thank you for finding and breaking up this religious terror cell right in our midst. Too bad so many got away, but I assume you have got them on the run, and they will soon be eliminated as a threat."

"Yes, Lady Crestoff. We are making great strides on that as we speak," replied Major Arson.

"I was happy to meet with you, but my time is limited. Is there something else you wished to speak with me about?" asked Lady Crestoff rather abruptly.

"If I may. I believe that there is more than just one of these religious terror cells. We are learning that they organize and meet in unusual places such as parking garages, forests, and even work camps. They have bold recruiters and use primitive ways of communicating which are difficult to trace. They are also faithful to their cause, even until death. This makes it difficult to find them and eliminate them," said Major Arson and then paused for effect.

"What would you suggest?" asked Lady Crestoff, hoping to hurry Major Arson to her point.

"I would like to propose chips to be mandatory. So these people would be easier to locate. Failure to comply would result in a prison sentence for them and their immediate family members. They don't mind self-sacrifice, but they don't want others to have to suffer. I would also suggest all religious terror cell leaders be sentenced to public execution for crimes against our government. This would discourage these groups from arising and would no longer cost the country so much of its time and resources."

Lady Crestoff looked out at her grand mountains. "I was hoping not to go this route. The world does not accept such things. Other countries will impose sanctions, and the world media will begin to do stories on these Ints and ignore the good we do for our people. The peace we've restored to this country will be overshadowed by this intolerant population. Public executions would be even worse. Maybe just local public executions that are unannounced. The world media would destroy us for public executions. I will have to weigh this carefully. And I suppose you would want to lead this up? Here in Denver? How many people would you need?" inquired Lady Crestoff, resting her gaze back on Major Arson.

"I think I would be the natural choice. If I were here in Denver, you could better oversee and advise on situations. I would need forty people," said Major Arson confidently.

"I will speak with you tomorrow at two," said Lady Crestoff.

"Thank you, Lady Crestoff," said Major Arson with a grateful smile.

"Thank you, for your service, Major Arson," replied Lady Crestoff.

And Lady Crestoff exited out the door her assistant held for her.

CHAPTER 29

And God is able to bless you abundantly, so that
in all things at all times, having all that you need,
you will abound in every good work.
2 Corinthians 9:8

The next morning at 8 a.m., after the morning worship and devotional time, Marcos arrived in his white Silverado pick-up. His square-toed cowboy boots clunked along as he walked. He was a broad-shouldered man, with dark pitted skin. His frisky eyes hid beneath the brim of his cowboy hat. Dante welcomed him with his booming voice and warm personality. Then he hollered across the crowded metal building for Stephen, Mark and Kendall.

The men were anxious to see the ranch and meet with Jeffrey Scheffron from SCIRO. They climbed in the pickup and barreled off the airstrip down a dirt road for about fifteen minutes. Marcos entered the sprawling ranch, and the men followed. A grand limestone fireplace centered on the far wall, and the adjacent wall was lined with wood framed windows that displayed rocky hills, scraggly bushes, cacti, and orange earth.

Jeffrey was at a large roughed out wooden table at the center of the room. It was at least sixteen feet long, and he had computers and monitors of all sizes and shapes scattered across the length of the table. Red, blue, white, and yellow wires, cords, and boxes were everywhere. When Jeffrey saw the men enter, he stood up. He was every bit as tall as Mark, but twice the shoulder width. He was in his forties, but his eyes were sprite as a child's. You could see the brilliance bubbling beneath them. Far from the tired eyes of the average IT guy and the typical antisocial computer nerd, Jeffrey welcomed the men with enthusiasm.

Jeffrey tried to explain simply the brilliant project he was working on. Mark, Stephen, and Kendall listened intently. Mark had to stop Jeffrey several times and ask him to clarify things. "So you've found a way to make a new bandwidth using the same fiber optics that's already running all through the country. But we can communicate on it without the government detecting us using it? Right?"

"Right!" responded Jeffrey, who was encouraged by their understanding.

"Why are you doing this? You know people who support this have died already? I mean you're a genius.

You're rich, or you should be. Why risk all of it? It's not even your country," asked Kendall, genuinely curious about Jeffrey's role in all of this.

"Well, I'm officially doing this because a shell company is paying me to do it. Technically, I'm doing this because the Australian government is paying me to do it, because they want to support a subversive democratic group whose government has been usurped by a communist party. They want to enable the nationalists to take back their country and return it the great democratic country that it once was. The greatest country that ever existed! What better reason could there be to die? I can't fire a gun, but I can take a whole nation down with a little electricity. This is going to be spectacular!" said Jeffrey with a wild look in his eyes.

The men paused just to see if he was being facetious or not. When he looked at them, genuinely looking for their acceptance, they all smiled in agreement. Mark and Jeffrey continued to talk about dates and uses and interfaces.

Marcos grabbed Kendall and Stephen and stepped out on the back porch. Marcos, in his thick Latino accent, said to the men, "Today's a very important, a sensitive shipment is coming. We will need to get all the men to be there to unload it and get it under cover as quickly as possible. There is a second hangar a half mile east. That is where we will store the supplies. But the plane will need to land on this airstrip. So I need your men to unload the plane and load the semis. It will be too much to carry the half mile. The plane will land at 1 p.m. I will take you back to speak to your men about this and to take the lunches for the men. I will bring Mark back later."

"What's on the plane, and where is it coming from?" asked Kendall as he touched the brim of his cowboy hat to tip it down to block the rising sun.

"It is a cargo plane from the Australian government," said Marcos as he looked at the men's reactions. They looked at Marcos surprised.

"Yes," said Marcos. "You men are having quite a yoke thrust upon you. The cargo plane contains forty military men to train your men, weapons, night gear, uniforms, drones, computer equipment, communications equipment, and two King Stallion helicopters."

"What? Two helicopters? What?" said Kendall, removing his hat, completely flabbergasted.

"We are going to need to pray and fast tonight," said Stephen, clearly taken aback. Kendall had never seen Stephen look shaken. "I can't go forward without the Lord before us and behind us, directing our path," said Stephen soberly.

"I agree," said Kendall.

"I agree, too," said Marcos. "I will join you this evening. Let's get back to the men, or rather the troops. We have much to tell them."

At 1 p.m., the sun blazed one hundred degrees Fahrenheit. Mirages and waves of heat could be seen down the airstrip. A group of nearly five hundred men lined the small airstrip. In the distance, the men saw a grey, Lockheed C-5 Galaxy appear in the sky. It was going to be a difficult landing for such a behemoth vehicle on a such a small airstrip. The engines roared in protest as they slowed and landing gears clunked open. As this beast landed precariously on this small airstrip, so did the hopes of these men, that one day they would once again be the land of the free, home of the brave.

Grant was sipping piping hot coffee when Genesis finally woke up. She rolled over on her pallet on the floor, surprised by the crowd that had gathered. Grant was looking at her, over his coffee cup. Levi was on the other side of her just staring at her, and Everest smiled at Gen as she shut her notebook that was nearly full now of bowing, bending, used pages. Grant set his cup of coffee down and said, "Gen, can we take a walk? I have many things I need to talk with you about."

"Give me ten minutes," she said with a smile.

They walked out back to rich farmland. The green corn was about knee high. The dirt beneath it was a deep moist brown. Caleb had told Grant of a path in the pines to the left of the barn that he and Anna had worn out over the years. Grant and Gen headed that way. The air was cool under the pine trees. Grant grabbed her hand and told her of the phone calls he had been receiving since Michelle Brice had been taken in as a political refugee at the British consulate in Houston, Texas. He had spoken to leaders in Iceland, Australia, and Britain. He told her of the communications system and the cargo shipment from Australia. He told her about the upcoming training for the men who were in Louisiana but were now in Texas. He told her of the plan for the temporary leadership for Mexico, Canada, and the United States.

Genesis, gasped. "What? Are you leaving?" asked Genesis.

"Soon. Yes," confirmed Grant.

"But what about the rest of us?" she asked.

Grant stopped walking and grabbed both of Genesis' hands and looked at her. He said, "I'm not sure what Mike and his wife will do, but he has many, many friends. God will show him what to do. I need Everest to go with me. She has proven herself invaluable to me in the last twenty-four hours. She keeps me organized and moving forward and keeps meticulous notes for me, and she prays for me without me even asking. Little Lissa is an unknown. I cannot take her with me where I am going, and yet I feel responsible for her."

"What about the Caleb and Anna? Would they take her in and adopt her as their own? Anna was so taken with her. She's breast feeding her, you know. Isn't that precious?" said Genesis.

Grant hesitated and then said, "Yes, of course. That is why God has directed our path here." He looked up briefly, thankful that the Lord was always one step ahead of him. Then Grant looked back at Genesis.

"Genesis, I don't want to seem presumptuous. I've known you such a short time. I don't know if I'll even live through the things that God has called me to do, but I know, without a doubt in my heart, I don't want to spend a day on this earth without you." He pulled Genesis up close to him and said, "Will you marry me? Will you marry me today? Under these pines, in a strange land, without our families, without our friends, just you and me. That's all I need. Just you and me." He searched her eyes and waited. Looking for any signs of doubt or pressure.

"Yes, yes, yes." Genesis said. And she pressed into his strong body as she kissed him; the smell of coffee and pine trees forever burnt in her memory.

That evening, in the cool canopy of the pines and the soft needle-covered ground, Pastor Mike married Grant and Genesis. Genesis' face was yellowing where the bruises were beginning to heal. Her clothes were the same ones purchased two days prior at a Walmart on the way to Montana. Grant was still in fatigues that represent a country he wouldn't claim as his own. His beard was thickening, and his hair was long. There were no rings, no pictures, no music, no chairs or decorations. Genesis and Grant knelt before Pastor Mike. They confessed their love and devotion first to Jesus their King and then to one another.

Darrell finally arrived at the Panther Refugee Camp. It was more like a small town now than a refugee camp. Cheyenne was the unelected leader. Her qualities of integrity, fairness, and intelligence made her the natural choice. She had a group of men and women that served alongside of her in the camp of about a thousand people. She no longer lived with her indigenous people, but felt most at home among the refugees, although she remained close with her tribe.

When Darrell arrived on foot, he was exhausted, dehydrated, and gaunt. Cheyenne was standing outside the community building at the center of the town.

When she saw him, he smiled at her faintly and stopped in his tracks. She was more breathtaking than he had remembered. Then he collapsed on the dirt path. Cheyenne turned and ran to him, calling his name. Lorenzo was outside working in a garden and heard her cry Darrell's name. Lorenzo went running to find him. Lorenzo and another man carried him to Cheyenne's quarters.

She, like all the others here, lived in a one room home. She slept in a hammock that stretched across the room at night. She had a water bowl for washing and a wood burning stove for eating and heating. There was a modest, handcrafted table with two chairs in one corner. Some children stopped in to see how Darrell was doing. She had them run and gather corn husks and blankets to build a pallet for him.

She washed his rich skin that was earth and strength to her. She gently changed his clothes. She noticed the healed cuts around his eyes and his mouth and the dark bruising around his ribs. She got rags from neighbors and wrapped them tightly around his ribs. She placed her hands on his ribs and prayed for the Lord to complete his healing. To make him as new physically as he had already done spiritually. She thanked the Lord for answering her prayers and bringing him back to her, the man she loved so dearly.

After a day of restate nourishment, Darrell was up and walking around the camp, enjoying all the new developments they had made since he had left. Darrell sat down with Lorenzo and Cheyenne over some hot coffee, and Lorenzo told Darrell of the grace God had shown the group for the rest of the journey. Then Darrell told Lorenzo and Cheyenne of the grand glimpses the Lord had shown Grant for the future of their countries and the roles each of them would play.

Later that evening, Cheyenne and Darrell walked arm in arm and step in step, talking some more about all that had happened since they last saw one another. He promised her this was the last time he would leave her. He wanted to speak with her father and tell him of the plans for their country, of the prophecy given, and especially the love he has for his daughter. Cheyenne would not marry Darrell without her father's approval. They had appealed to him before with no avail. Darrell said, "This time, Cheyenne, it is different. I feel it in my Spirit. It is not your life I will beg him for. This time it is for his life. It is not me that your father rejects. It is Jesus. We will pray and fast. Then we will go see him. And you, Cheyenne, will be my wife at last." He ran his hands down her long, silk hair and kissed her forehead, her ears, her lips, and forgot about all the pain of yesterdays and the imposing tomorrows.

CHAPTER 30

May he give you the desire of your heart and make
all your plans succeed.
Psalm 20:4

Six Months Later

Grant, Cheyenne, and Lorenzo stood around the large wooden table at the center of the great room at the ranch. They had spent hours poring over the floor plans of the presidential building in Denver, Colorado. Grant finally stood up straight and stretched his back. Lorenzo followed suit, resting his hands on his waist. Cheyenne, though, continued tenaciously looking at the details of the entrances, the staff offices, the placement of guards, snipers, cameras, secret services. Then she shuffled through the schedules of the staff and security. "I still think that our best point of entry is the roof. It gives us the least casualties and the best element of surprise."

The three leaders standing, looking at one another, were powerful, knowledgeable, and confident. They had been through months of legal, military, and leadership training. They were not the same people they were six months ago. They trained spiritually in the mornings. They fasted and sought God together three times a week. They trained late into the night physically. But during the day, they poured over histories of governments that had changed over and coups, both violent and peaceful. They studied in great depth even the takeover of their own countries by the current communist government.

Genesis walked in the front door with a box of seven satellite phones. Her blonde dreads were back, along with her feistiness after her long ordeal back in Minnesota. She set the phones down and stood beside her husband. Darrell entered moments later with Stephen.

"Could I have everyone take a seat, and I will go over the plans for Resurgence Day," requested Stephen. He glanced up and smiled as Mark and Kendall joined them and quietly grabbed a seat. Stephen ran his hand unconsciously over his newly cut, military style hair. It tamed his bright red hair tone but brought out his steely blue eyes and gave him a new fierce angular appearance. His black t-shirt hugged his new physic which had morphed from a large farm boy to an intimidating military figure. He looked at his comrades with admiration and love. "Let's begin on our knees as only appropriate." The warriors in all humility went straight to their knees. "Lord Jesus, we are here only because you have brought us here. We are here to retrieve what has been stolen. Be glorified in all that we do. We beseech You King of all kings, to grant us Your favor in the complex mission set before us. Ride out before us, Holy Spirit, be among us and guard us from behind. Amen," declared Stephen.

Stephen flipped open the computer, and his screen mirrored vibrantly onto the wall behind him. "We have had many obstacles to overcome. Most would say they were insurmountable obstacles. But our group of military recruits in Texas has gone from five hundred men to over two thousand men and women. Each going through bootcamp, followed by rigorous training in special skills needed to make a working military. The Canadian camp in Fort Hope now have a whopping four thousand men and women being trained by a military group from Iceland. Many of these men and women are new believers. Mexico has been devastated with drought and famine over the last two years. Its people are struggling in every way. But, praise God, Mexico's camp now has one thousand men and women.

"On Resurgence Day, we will be taking custody of six buildings simultaneously. All six buildings have completely different set ups.

"Building one: The Beale Air Force Base in Marysville, California. It is one of the largest bases. It covers twenty-three thousand acres. There is just one building we will be taking. We will approach by truck. It is a two-story building. We have five loyal informants at the very top of the chain there. We will be coordinating every step with them in order to ensure as few lives are lost as possible. They will also be feeding us minute by minute intel.

"Building two: The Watervliet Arsenal in Watervliet, New York. It is a small one-story building. We will take it by land with trucks. We have ten loyal followers of Jesus there. They will be strategically placed at the entrance, the manufacturing plant, the research facility, and the armory.

"Building three: the former White House in the District of Columbia. It will not be difficult to take. As we have all seen, the beloved home of our former government that was of the people, for the people and by the people was burned and looted during the riots and left to stand in ruins. It is a disgrace and used by our current government as a reminder that they have destroyed our old way of life, and they will destroy anyone who dares come against them. We are going to restore and once again open the halls of the White House and fill it with free Americans. We will rebuild while presidential candidates run for office to once again be elected by citizens to represent what their states believe. At the White House, we will once again open with prayer, hang the Ten Commandments, and read aloud our constitution regularly so we never again forget the freedoms we have once again fought for."

Stephen turned to find every one of his American comrades standing and weeping in remembrance of what a great nation they once were. As he looked at them, they all began clapping, then cheering, then praising God for this opportunity to become one nation under God, indivisible with liberty and justice for all, once again.

Stephen continued, and the group of men and women sat back down. "Building four: the current center of our government, The Glass House in Denver, Colorado. This building will be, by far, the most difficult to penetrate. It is a predominantly glass building. It is four stories high. The Grand Windowed Office is on the fourth floor. The only way we have to enter is by air. We have eight people inside the building, but they are all at lower levels. The President and the majority of the secret service will be in New York at the time of entry, but there is still a remnant of secret service people that will be in the building. This is what we've been training for.

"Building five: the Parliament of Canada at Parliament Hill, Ottawa. This again is a deserted, dilapidated building. It will not be difficult to take but is essential to restoring Canada to a sovereign nation once again.

"Building Six: the National Palace in Mexico City, Mexico. This is the most disheartening task before us. This beautiful, historical building that once was the vibrant heart of Mexico is now being used as a morgue, due to the recent famine. We will need to deal with this building from the grassroots level slowly. The bodies need to be buried or cremated and treated with dignity with family notifications and ceremonies. We don't know the condition of the building or the bodies. We will be taking disease experts, medical experts, and a small amount of military and translators. We will also have a camera crew to record and assure the public that we are taking care of their loved ones. But this building must be recovered for the establishment of the sovereign government of Mexico.

"As you know, Grant will be the leader of the United States until a President is elected. Cheyenne will lead Canada and Lorenzo will leas Mexico. Mexico will need lots of prayer and aid to get her back up on her feet. Each of these countries will need to establish a Congress or Parliament as soon as possible. I will be at the Beale Air Force Base running the ops from there. I will be leading the military until the newly elected President appoints someone.

"Then our Australian friend Jeffrey will take over news, radio, television, and internet and broadcast a message to America, Mexico, and Canada, inviting them to embrace freedom once again. There will be a special way for police and military to respond. There will be Australian and European forces occupying our country after these buildings are secured and our police and military gathered. They will help organize and distribute them as well as securing dissenters.

"We will be studying these operations in great detail, step by step, minute by minute, over and over in the next week with our allied military experts. This is just your first overview. Any questions?"

Cheyenne spoke up. "How did we get these floor plans, schedules, and rosters of the new presidential quarters in Denver?" Stephen, looked away, out the window into the dry land, and remembered the details relayed to him. He replied sadly, "It came at a great cost."

CHAPTER 31

*Do not take revenge, my dear friends, but leave
room for God's wrath, for it is written: "It is mine
to avenge; I will repay," says the Lord.*
Romans 12:19

Meagan's autumn shaded hair cascaded down her back in beautiful long rolls. She worked her way across the room to her other heel that laid tossed on its side and worked it back onto her foot. She seethed at the man across the room from her as he primped himself in the mirror.

"I hate you, Elliot," her hazel eyes flashed at him. "One day, you will pay for this."

"Oh please, don't be so dramatic Meagan," he replied. It's not like I hurt you. Look at these scratches." Elliot tipped his chin up and winced as he touched the three thin stripes by his collar bone.

"You raped me," she whispered under her breath.

"Oh, now we're going to point out each other's wrongs. Your list of sins is plenty long, Meagan, dear. What is it you need this file for did you say?" questioned Elliot, suspiciously. He turned to her as he buttoned his shirt, and she intuitively stepped back, pulling her dress down quickly and pulling at the back zipper, clearly flustered. "Here, now let me help you with that, so you can see what a gentleman I am, and so you quit using nasty words like that "r" word." He walked her back up against the wall and reached around her and slowly pulled the zipper up the back of the dress. He relished Meagan's trembling as he did this. "There you go, Meagan. Let me know if you need anything else. I'm always eager to help, but please remember, nothing is free in this world." He picked up his suit coat and tie, threw it over his arm and exited the room.

Meagan sunk to the floor and wept as whispers flooded her ears with promises. "Be strong, do not fear; your God will come, He will come with vengeance; with divine retribution He will come to save you."

———————————————————————

Elliot entered the windowed office of Lady Crestor. His hair was neatly combed to the side, his red tie was snuggly in place, and his suit coat lay neatly over the three small streaks of blood on his pressed white shirt.

"Madame President, here are the talking points you requested for the press conference with United Arab Nation's president. It highlights, of course, your accomplishments in the negotiations: the separation of religion and state, the state perimeters over religious activities, and the control and monitoring of assemblies and the press. As the world looks upon our success, they will be eager to adopt constitutions similar to ours. Then, you will paint the picture of a world at peace, united and strong, equal in all ways. Surely, Europe will be next to join us."

Lady Crestoff paced restlessly across the wood floors before the grand windows. The mountains stood at attention just beyond, guarding the Lady herself. "Has Major Arson had any success yet with this rogue group of Ints? I cannot be made a fool on the brink of this momentous, global conference!" She spun about so quickly that Elliot had to suppress his startle reflex. He tried not to stammer and yet tried not to exaggerate or speak something into existence just to appease Lady Crestoff's growing anger, knowing that others had perished for doing so.

"That is not my area of council, and we met this morning and Gregg did not report any new info..."

She cut off his last word and shouted, "What do you think? Is our house in order? Will I be made a fool of in front of the world? Isn't it clear what I am asking?"

"Of course, you are no fool, Lady Crestoff. You are the prominent leader of this world. All look to your wisdom. You have been aggressive in cutting off any Ints and their families from interfering with our peaceful society, and you have done so with great patience and wisdom. You have given them every opportunity and incentive to join us. But, at every turn, they have rejected us. They are not right in the mind as you know. These concerns are real. Every government will be facing the same dilemmas. They will look to you for the answers to these problems. This is the exact moment in history when your genuine concern for the multitudes and your transparency with our own problems with Ints could pave the way to force all citizens to take the chip. We could show the world how to do it."

"And how do we accomplish that?" she asked, fully engaged in his line of reasoning.

"We drive them to ask for it. No Int would ask for the mark, but they would if we tied it to the purchase of everything. We can do away with currency. Tie everything to the electric transfer of funds through our federal banks, which we are most of the way there already, and only those chipped would be able to buy anything: homes, cars, gas, food, clothing, phones, electricity, medicine. Ints would die for their cause but would they slowly starve? Would they watch their children starve when there is perfectly good food down the street waiting for them? We would make it clear once and for all that we want to help them, but it is their choice. They have to want to receive this free gift of life we are offering. We will shower them with rewards, get them back on their feet again, and rejoice with them when they return to their beloved country once again. This is the way to peacefully transfer the misplaced power of a divided people to the power of a united government that is for the people."

The room was quiet for a long moment. "You are suggesting we announce our plans for chipping all of our people at these accords?"

"Yes, Lady President. I am." Elliot pronounced boldly.

"Yes. Yes. I believe you're right. This is the precise time. Add it to the presentation and get a report to me stating what resources are needed to see this accomplished."

Lady Crestoff spoke quietly to herself as Elliot listened in. "It has been years of patiently, dealing with these stiff necked Ints and their mythology. They will come to our reality or they will come to their ends by their own hands. Oh, how I've hated their rebellion against me. They are a stain, a virus that has dogged my presidency long enough. The world leaders will all have to deal with the plague, and I will show them how to finish it, and then the world will be united at peace, and they will worship me for what I've given them."

Lady Crestoff ran her hands over her smooth, pinned back hair and silently turned back to the window. Elliot watched as the Lady inhaled and drew herself up even taller than her full six-foot stature. "Make it so in the speech. It is time. And get me Major Arson in here," Lady Crestoff demanded.

CHAPTER 32

But he was pierced for our transgressions, he was crushed for our iniquities; the punishment that brought us peace was on him, and by his wounds we are healed.
Isaiah 53:5

Meagan juggled the pen, the waters, and the other things in her hands while balancing the large bag of laptops thrown over her shoulder, all while in heels. The sprite, clicking of her heels echoed down the hallway. She was behind schedule. She glanced at the door ahead of her and was glad to see Agent Mitch approach just in time to open the door for her. He didn't make any eye contact with Meagan but surveyed the hallway, the exits, and the other doors as he opened it. He touched his com in his ear and whispered something cryptic. Then watched Meagan, unbeknownst to her, as she bent to release the bag of computers. New York was a wretched town, but it still was the epicenter for the United Nations. The self-absorbed New Yorkers made her feel like an insecure school child all over again.

She hurried over to adjust the chairs and mics. She straightened the rug. Then she spun around and studied the room. "This is the most important meeting of my lifetime. And it must go off like we've done it ten thousand times." The crisp, threatening words of Lady Crestoff echoed in her mind. She walked purposefully over to a lamp and straightened the shade. It wasn't a glamorous job, but she had worked her whole life to get here and did plenty of unscrupulous things to get to this job. It certainly wasn't her family connections that got her this job. Meagan had come from humble beginnings that embarrassed her as a child, repulsed her as a teenager, and drove her to success through college. Her ambition and lack of scruples took her the rest of the way.

Meagan practiced the walk of each of the Arab representatives and then the final entry of the Lady herself. She knew that having the host enter last was not traditional and edgy, to say the least, but it sent a message of power and confidence in this humble entrance. Like a bride veiled and last to enter but clearly the cynosure. She smiled to herself. It was the first time in days that she able to lose herself enough in something that she could forego the recent horror. And just that quickly, its memory threatened to drop her to her knees. His shoulder glancing off her cheek bone. His ferocious grunting and the smell of onions in his sweat. She gasped for air. She felt the sour, warm liquid creep up her throat and she searched for an object in the room to grasp or at least to steady her eyes on.

"Miss. Miss! Meagan? Are you all right?"

She felt herself sway ever so slightly, then she felt a hand on her side, and she leapt away and screamed.

Mitch touched his com and muttered something, and two more agents entered the other doors.

"Meagan. It's okay. It's okay." She looked at Mitch and then sank to the floor in his arms. There were muttering and footsteps then darkness and whispers; the whispers again. "I am here. Do not be afraid. I will never leave you."

The Secret Service agents seamlessly covered for Mitch in his absence. They relished his presence being gone because he frankly creeped the other agents out. Mitch accompanied Meagan to the NYU ER, although he was of little help to the paramedics. He didn't know much about Meagan other than her heart-stopping poise and unusual beauty. He had to purpose himself not to stare and often failed. She was a loner to a point of arousing suspicion but seemed to be trusted in the inner circle of Lady Crestoff's staff. All of this was use-less information to the paramedics working on her.

Mitch was given a small conference room to wait in at the NYU ER since he was part of the President's staff. While he waited in the dimly lit room, he called back to Denver to gather info on Meagan so he could contact her family. He was surprised to learn there wasn't any family to telephone. No children, no husband, father unknown, mother was deceased, no sisters or brothers, and the emergency contact listed was not answering. He looked at his watch and searched the empty room for answers. When none could be found, he placed a knee on the floor. Someone walking by might have mistaken this large man for a coach taking a knee to describe a crucial play to eager players at the turning point of a game. But no players were to be found. One might think his deep set, dark eyes were beseeching his true love's hand in marriage, but it couldn't be so because his shoulders were slouched with uncertainty. But if one could hear his whispers, his words, the con-versation and pauses, someone would think he was speaking with a father, a brother, or a dear friend. The tenderness and familiarity would've moved one to lean closer in, to desire to hear what Mitch was hearing. It would make any grown man desire this intimacy and trust and comradery that he had. This relationship that seemed so reliable and real and so readily available. So bewilderingly strange to see a grown man in this manner. He would be thought half mad and yet the sanest of all. Such a dichotomy and mystery this scene would cause. Then at once, Mitch stood and moved through the doorway with purpose.

And there he sat in Meagan's hospital room in the green, vinyl chair with his glasses perched on the tip of his nose, reading aloud from the Bible on his phone, completely unconcerned about any possible consequences. He paused occasionally and looked at her tranquil form on the bed. Her opaque skin was a little paler than usual. Her arms appeared a little thinner. Her hand laid limp on the colorless blankets. Then he began to read again. He would stop when he was led to expound on the wonders of the Lord's love for his people and the lengths that He goes to rescue them from themselves and their enemies. His voice was like a song in the room, singing her back to health physically and spiritually.

CHAPTER 33

And Elisha prayed, "Open his eyes, Lord, so that
he may see." Then the Lord opened the servant's
eyes, and he looked and saw the hills full of horses
and chariots of fire all around Elisha.
2 Kings 6:17

Mitch was summoned back to work the following day. The other agents would stay in New York for two more days until the conference was finished. The President had two more speaking engagements and three more public meals on the schedule. It was important to the safety of the President to have as little variation to the agents as possible, so Mitch was to return to the President's Palace in Denver to prepare with team B agents for return of Lady Crestoff. Mitch's responsibilities were always on Door One, meaning Mitch was always just outside whatever door that Lady Crestoff was inside working. He was never on residential duties, only working duties. Mitch's sign was "the seer" and that's why he had Door One. The agents always ensured, wherever the President was working, there were multiple doors in and out of the room. Mitch was in charge of Door One. That was the main entrance in and out. If danger entered, it was Mitch's fault. Mitch had been known to have some "spiritual connection" to evil because he could sense it and was known to not let certain people enter the President's work area. The secret service did their background checks, but Mitch had his own checking system, and no one questioned it. He had personally averted two assassination attempts and thwarted one poisoning attempt, not to mention dozens of covert operations. The First Lady trusted his judgment without question. But to the team of agents, he was weird and out of cinque with the group. They didn't understand him, nor did they want to.

It was 4 a.m., and the First Lady and her team would be returning tomorrow at 1 p.m. It should've been an easy day checking schedules and visitors, meetings, entrances and exits but something was amiss. He slept fitfully last night and was aroused to pray in the Spirit on and off. He counted the paces to the First Lady's desk again and again. He checked the windows and his paces to and from every door. He checked for the hidden weapons in the room. He checked the ventilation, the cameras again and again. It was not physical. It was spiritual. He had never done this before. There were cameras everywhere, but he walked around the borders of the rectangular room, praying until the morning light shined threw the windows. The other agents had picked up on Mitch's body language. They saw his pacing, his checking and double checking, and that confounded muttering he does to himself. Finally, one of the other agents approached him.

"What is your problem, Mitch?" he asked in an accusing tone. "You've got everyone jumpy."

"The First Lady is coming back tomorrow at one, right? The itinerary hasn't changed?" asked Mitch.

"No. And you've checked that twice already. Geez. Relax," said the other agent.

"I want to know if anything changes. Is there anything on the schedule for this room today?" inquired Mitch, trying to sound a little less anxious.

"No, but Elliot and Gregg came back a day early, and I assume they might use the room to work on the speech for the Nation's Address about dealing with the Ints."

"No." Mitch said a little too aggressively. "I don't want them or anyone else in this room today. Understood?"

"I'll tell Elliot, but he might not like it. That prick thinks he's running the place."

"Just send him to me if he gives you any flack," replied Mitch.

"Is it the Meagan chick? Is that what's got you all messed up? I heard you spent time with her in the hospital. She's not your type, Mitch. You don't get out much, do you? Just relax. Today's supposed to be an easy day for the guys, and you've got everybody all uptight." The agent shook his head and walked away.

"Maybe he's right. I just got to relax. I didn't get enough sleep last night," Mitch thought to himself. "Lord, You are my refuge and my strength. I will rely on You. Come, Holy Spirit. All other spirits go." And Mitch breathed in, and... "Wait. Watch. See. I am doing a new thing."

Mitch looked one last time at every item in the room. It was empty and still. He walked out of the room and closed the door. He stood dutifully in front of Door One, guarding nothing. Or so he thought. "Those who are with us are more than those who are with them." Mitch quickened in his Spirit and beseeched the Lord out loud, "Open my eyes, Lord, that I may see!"

Elliot and Gregg rounded the corner and walked down the hall toward Mitch, chatting eagerly about the changes and potential pitfalls awaiting their young nation. Mitch looked up to see them approach and tried to hide his scowl.

Elliot tried his best disarming smile. "How ya doing, Mitch? We were just..."

Mitch's eye darted up as he heard a subtle thump, thump, thump. His mind rushed through possibilities: workmen, not on schedule; helicopter, protected airspace; weapons, wrong rhythm and pitch: helicopters. His hand went to his com as he entered the room. He hadn't noticed Elliot's and Gregg's minds coming to similar conclusions shortly after his had. They intuitively followed Mitch into the room. Four succinct hollow plops hit the grand window. All three of their heads spun to see the grey clay matter suctioned to the bullet proof twelve-inch thick glass.

"Bomb!" Mitch yelled as three of the other entrance doors burst open, and three additional agents entered the room with guns drawn. But, as they rushed forward, they were thrown backwards by the explosions. Guns thrust out of their hands. Arms flying backwards. Bodies thrown against walls. Mitch watched as shards of glass flew about soundlessly in slow motion. He landed on top of Gregg, crushing Gregg's shoulder to the ground. Mitch heard again more forcefully than before, "See!"

And at that moment came chariots and horses aflame through the window. They skidded to stops. The horses neighed violently and scuffed their hoofs. The chariots pushed and maneuvered around each other. The horses leapt in anticipation of war. The flames licked the drapes and roused with the wind from the open window, but Mitch stared in wonderment and fear as nothing caught fire. Mitch turned and saw no one else gaping at the sight. Mitch was still disoriented from the blast, but he saw more agents now entering the room with weapons drawn. They were on their coms looking up. They began shouting and pointing and dispersing. Mitch's hearing began to return but was muffled. As the smoke cleared, he watched the horses and chariots fade from his sight. Then, through the settling debris and smoke, four ropes brought four swinging men through the broken shards of glass. Mitch saw it then, as clear as he saw the gun outstretched before him in his hand, flames of fire resting on the heads of each man.

Elliot was the first to drop. The first bullet hit to the right of his groin, and the second went through his heart. Gregg no sooner stood up then was jerked back three times by three bullets shot in his torso three times. Mitch turned to see them fall, but then his training kicked in. Bullets were flying in all directions the worst of situations. Mitch fired and aimed, but his gun jammed. He rolled behind a large desk and flipped it for cover. He saw agent after agent look desperately at their jammed guns. One by one, the agents fell. More agents entered, and a few of their shots went off and two of the four intruders went down. The agents' guns began to jam again. Curses and anger and desperation filled the room. Still Mitch's gun was jammed as he stayed behind cover. Another bullet rang out, and the third intruder dropped to his knees, injured. A moment of peace in the midst of so much death. Mitch bravely stood gun down and walked toward the final intruder that was still standing.

Grant yelled to Mitch, "I need to secure the room. We need to secure it. You're going to have to help me get to these doors and secure it." Just then another agent entered, and Grant dropped him. Mitch looked at Grant and the flame about his head and said, "I've got your back."

Then, Grant and Mitch, back pressed to back, walked over dead and injured bodies from door to door, taking out the enemies as they approached. Mitch was surprised, only for a moment, to find that his gun was operational now. Together, the two men of God secured the Grand Windowed Office as rebel troops poured onto the roof tops and into every floor of the Glass House.

LIST OF CHARACTERS

Genesis McGuffey: Member of the Partakers

Grant Panther: Leader of the Partakers

Dr. Houston: The doctor at East Bank Hospital performing organ removals on Ints

Everest: Receptionist at East Bank Hospital and Partaker

Darrell Drake: Member of the Partakers

Lorenzo: Member of the Partakers

Boxer: Member of the Partakers

Major Asia Arson: Military leader at the ACI Americas Communist Investigations

Lieutenant Commander Michelle Brice: highest military leader at ACI

Officer Wong: Vietnamese officer serving under Major Arson

Private Neil: Major Arson's administrative assistant

Trevor and Autumn: Parents traveling to refugee camp with baby Lissa

Matthew and Ashley: Parents traveling to refugee camp with their four boys, Judah, Luke, Paul, and Peter

Devon and Trina: Parents traveling to refugee camp with their thirteen-year-old daughter Makayla

Gretchen Rueport: HR person at Children's Hospital

Dianne: HR person at East Bank Hospital

Aarav: Custodian at Children's Hospital

Mark: Smuggles Bibles into the Beaumont Work Camp for the Kingdom Workers

Juan and Maria: Their son Miguel is a patient at Children's Hospital

Kendall Ledbetter: Runs Work Camp #07

Stephen: Leader of the Kingdom Workers at Work Camp #07

Breelyn: Play therapist at Children's Hospital

Barbara: The nurse that took Darrel, Trevor, Autumn, and baby Lissa in

Dianne: HR director at East Bank Hospital

Cindy: Dr. Houston's nurse

Jin: Chipped Asian woman aiding the Partakers

Matthew Raven: Famous American actor

Marcos: Runs Matthew Raven's ranch

Dante: Worship leader of the Kingdom Workers

Caleb and Anna: An Amish couple; friends of Grant's

Jeffrey Scheffron: IT genius from Australia

Lady Crestoff: Current president of the United Communist Americas

Meagan: One of the administrative assistants to Lady Crestoff

Elliot: Speech writer for Lady Crestoff

Mitch: Secret service agent

CPSIA information can be obtained
at www.ICGtesting.com
Printed in the USA
BVHW041721110521
607048BV00008B/2400

9 781637 691564